The Widow of Candleriggs

Jenny Telfer Chaplin

BeWrite Books

Published internationally by BeWrite Books, UK.
32 Bryn Road South, Wigan, Lancashire, WN4 8QR.

© Jenny Telfer Chaplin 2005

The right of Jenny Telfer Chaplin to be identified as the author has been asserted in accordance with sections 77 and 78 of the Copyright, Designs and Patents Act 1988. All rights reserved.

A CIP catalogue record for this book is available from the British Library

ISBN-10: 1-905202-22-9
ISBN-13: 978-1-905202-23-2

Also available in eBook format.

Produced by BeWrite Books

Jenny Chaplin, well known to loyal readers worldwide for her books on Scottish social history and for her articles in the *Scots Magazine* and the *Scottish Banner*, presents her first novel.

Jenny, as a Fellow of the Society of Antiquarians of Scotland, is well qualified to write her historical novels after years of research into and writing about Scottish social history.

She now writes her novels in her centuries old cottage on the Island of Bute under the name Jenny Telfer Chaplin to differentiate between her fiction and non-fiction writing.

Also by Jenny Chaplin:
Non-fiction
From Scotland's Past
A Glasgow Hogmanay
The Puzzle of Parkinson's
One Editor's Life
Alone in a Garden (Poetry Collection)
Thoughts on Writing (Co-authors: Fay Goldie & V. Cuthbert)

Fiction
The Kinnons of Candleriggs
Tales of a Glasgow Childhood
Childhood Days in Glasgow
Happy Days in Rothesay
We Belonged to Glasgow (An anthology)

The
Widow of Candleriggs

Part One

Chapter 1

Kate Rafferty Kinnon sat in her tenement home in Glasgow's Candleriggs and surveyed the remains of the funeral tea. Yes, as such events went, it had been a success. Pearce Claude Kinnon had indeed been given 'a grand send-off'.

Although, Kate thought ruefully, *with his being a non-believer in her own staunch Baptist faith, quite where in the universe or the great beyond he had been sent off to, was another matter. Still, the fact remained, Pearce had been a gentleman all his life – at least in the eyes of the rest of the world – so it had been fitting that in death, he had received the trappings appropriate to his genteel birth even if that had cost her every penny, and more, of the hoard of money Daniel had given to her after his visit to his father's relatives in Ireland. Money Pearce had forbidden Kate to use even for the necessities of life.*

With these thoughts racing through her brain, Kate let out a long sigh born of the frustration of what her own life had been with Pearce. On the point of going further down the twists and turns of memory lane, she was interrupted by a voice from the hall: "Coo-ee, Kate. It's only me."

In the overcrowded and rat-ridden Scottish tenements nobody ever locked a door and since friends came and went otherwise unannounced, it could have been any one of her near neighbours.

Kate dabbed at her eyes with an already sodden rag, sat up straighter, and prepared to pin a welcoming smile on her care-lined face.

Granny Gorbals, never one for false jollity, at once said: "Listen here, Katie, my girl. Ye're no needin tae stand on ceremony with me. If ye feel like howlin yer een oot, then for the sake of Mary, Joseph, and all the Angels, just get on with it."

Having delivered herself of this homily. Granny creaked her arthritic body over to the fireside where she placed a skeletal arm around Kate's shoulders. This simple yet comforting gesture was enough to open yet again the floodgates of emotion. Kate released the pent-up fears, misery, and utter frustration of her years of marriage with Pearce. As the scalding tears gushed from her eyes and poured down her face, she knew it was not only for the trauma of Pearce's death that she mourned. No! She was bewailing the passing of an era and the lingering, haunting regret left by years of marital disharmony. If only things could have been different! What if their once all-consuming passion of youth, hope, and expectancy had lasted. Even more, what if ...

Kate was saved further soul-destroying introspection when she felt a gentle pull at her sleeve and an enamel mug was placed in her hands, together with the words: "Drink that down ye, lass. A good strong cup of tea, it'll do ye good. And forbye, I've added a generous tot from the medicinal bottle."

At these words, Kate managed a wintry smile. She knew from past experience in dealing with the dramas of life in these crumbling Glasgow tenements, that the minute the carefully-hoarded medicinal bottle was produced from its habitual hiding place, then Granny Gorbals would be right there.

With this in mind, and ever-conscious of her duties as a Candleriggs neighbour, Kate managed to hold on to her hard-won smile. She leant forward and placed a hand on Granny's bowed shoulders.

"Granny! Ye surely cannot be thinking that I'll be drinking doctored tea all on my own. For the sake of your own beloved Saint Michael and all his Angels ... get yourself a tinny and join me."

Scarcely were the words out of Kate's mouth, than Granny Gorbals, arthritic limbs or not, bounded towards the bottle of good Scotch whisky with all the energy of a woman half her age. Then, having taken Kate entirely at her word, and leaving barely enough room in the mug for the tea itself, Granny carried her precious burden across the room. With due and proper respect for the solemnity of the occasion, Granny Gorbals settled herself in the chair which had once been the sole preserve of the master of the house.

Once settled, Granny Gorbals sipped at her mug of tea and with a smile of contentment, it was clear that she was enjoying to the full the luxury of the roaring fire, the inner glow of whisky, and her important, if self-imposed, role of comforter of the recently bereaved.

"Aye, lass. So, that's yer good man away to his eternal rest. God keep his soul. Well, he'll be in good company. Just imagine it. Our beloved Queen Victoria and Pearce arriving at the gates of heaven within the very same week."

With Granny's eyes taking on a faraway look, at once Kate had a mental picture of Pearce escorting a crowned and bejewelled Queen Victoria to the nearest heavenly cloud with its attendant harp-playing angel. It was all Kate could do to stifle a giggle.

In a bid to get over this, she said: "Put it this way, Granny. Pearce always did like to be in high society. So, what with Her Britannic Majesty on his arm and his floating around the realms of Heaven like the Laird he always imagined himself to be, he'll never get any grander or more regal than that."

Granny nodded in total agreement with this sentiment.

A silence hung between them until at last the old woman said: "Aye! But life goes on. There's still Hannah, Jenny, and Wee Theresa here at home with you. Not to mention your many bits of work outside. And you're not an old woman yet, Kate. You've a deal of living still to do ... and don't you ever forget it."

No sooner were these words spoken than Kate, with an inner

glow, not entirely due to the effect of the whisky, recalled her meeting with Terence O'Neil at the funeral tea.

As if almost reading her mind, Granny suddenly leant forward and, with the look of someone ready for a good old gossip, said: "Oh! I meant to ask ... and just who would that fine handsome Irishman be who appeared out of the blue?"

Determined to get a bit of fun and hopefully, at the same time, to send Granny off on a false trail, Kate said, with an exaggerated look of amazement: "My word, Granny, but you must be real desperate for a man if ye think old Shuggie to be a fine figure."

At once appreciating the joke, Granny gave a cackle which then grew to a real belly laugh.

"Katie Kinnon! You've got a real dirty mind if ye think a decent widow woman like myself would look that way at any man. After I planted my sainted Patrick in the Emerald Isle there was never anyone else for me. In any case, it wasnae old Shuggie I meant. It was the other one."

The mention of 'the other one' at once gave Kate a vivid mental image of Terence O'Neil with his book barrow. Yes, Granny was right.

"So, Granny. Ye've got a great taste in men. Indeed, a fine upstanding man. Aye, come to think of it, Terence O'Neil would be just grand for you."

When Jenny arrived home with Hannah and Theresa from their walk, it was to the sound of laughter as Granny Gorbals and Kate howled their merriment at their shared but secret joke.

Yes. Life would go on.

Chapter 2

The days following Pearce's funeral seemed to merge into one another.

Jenny's helpful demeanour and attitude, at least toward Kate, in the weeks leading up to Pearce's death deteriorated and Jenny slipped back to her old ways of questionable friends.

As Kate went about her day-to-day life in and around the Candleriggs, she was surrounded on all sides by buildings, shops and warehouses draped in black. To make matters even worse, not only were people cast in the mental gloom of mourning for Queen Victoria, but their already drab clothes were bedecked with black patches and clumsily cut-out cloth diamonds obviously hastily stitched on to jackets and sleeves. In keeping with this sombre mood, there was also a tangible fear abroad, fear of the unknown now that the old regime had gone, and the terror of the outbreak of smallpox then rampaging through the streets, wynds, and vennels of the City of Glasgow.

Kate shifted the burden of her shopping basket to her left hand. As she did so, the turnip which had been poised on top fell out and rolled along the gutter. With a tut of annoyance, Kate bent down to retrieve what would be the mainstay of the evening meal. But another hand had been quicker.

"Well, now, Mistress Kinnon. Are you not the fine lady with money to spare ... throwing good food away like this."

Kate raised her head to find herself gazing into the twinkling eyes of Terence O'Neil. In that instant, remembering the previous conversation with Granny Gorbals, she felt herself blushing furiously. In a vain bid to cover her confusion, she started babbling like an over-excited schoolgirl.

At last, Terence held up his hands in mock horror. "And I thought I was the one who had kissed the Blarney Stone."

Kate laughed. "Well, put it this way. Mister O'Neil, sir, according to my friend and neighbour Granny Gorbals, there's not a finer Irish gentleman than your good self ever kissed the Blarney Stone."

Scarcely were the words out of her mouth, than Kate blushed even deeper, horrified at her own lack of restraint.

What on earth would the man think of me? As if not bad enough dishing out compliments, here I was in one revealing sentence telling him that he was of sufficient importance to merit discussion with Granny.

But it was soon apparent from his delighted grin that rather than being shocked, the same Terence was enjoying to the full the luxury of being the centre of attention. And quick to press home his advantage, he said: "Now then, Mistress Kinnon, perhaps you would allow me to walk you safely home ... before you start throwing the rest of those vegetables from your basket at any other strange men. I've heard of you women fluttering down a handkerchief for male attention but vegetables? Never."

Kate chuckled and quickly entering the fun of the thing, said: "Now, since you mention it ... I don't know that I could do too much damage with what's left of my tuppence-worth of soup-pot vegetables. Anyway, come to think of it, I doubt I'd meet any man stranger than yourself."

As they laughed in happy unison and set off along the Trongate together, Kate was aware of a lightening of her heart and a renewed spring in her step. Certainly, the acres of black crepe still enshrouded Glasgow; the passing populace still looked as grey and miserable; and knots of worried citizens still spoke in reverential whispers about the spectre of Death with its lack of respect even for such a Lady of Quality as the old Queen herself and with its current largesse of the dreaded smallpox in their own midst. But Kate had a feeling that life had miraculously taken on the rainbow hues of hope.

But it would have taken an entire heaven of rainbows to lighten her mood next morning. In desperation she had taken a job as a rag picker. Initially she had taken on the vile job to enable her to buy the extras of decent food and small luxuries with which to brighten Pearce's last days on earth. From that point of view, the foul work had earned its keep. She had promised herself that once such dire need as Pearce's creature comforts had gone, so too would she herself be gone and out of the hell-hole as fast as her legs would carry her. But now, having lavishly overspent on Pearce's grand funeral she was in debt and her many small jobs – the twice weekly cleaning at Mrs Scott's, the early morning stint at the newsagent's, the close cleanings – came no place near to clearing the debts, paying the rent, and feeding Jenny, Theresa, and herself. So, here was she, still trapped in the role of rag picker.

Entering yet again the dim space between the arches of the railroad, she gagged at the smell of the place. It was damp, rat-ridden, and foul with the stench of old clothes stacked mountain-high awaiting the attention of the other women like Kate, whose job it was to sort through the detritus garnered from the populace of the City of Glasgow.

And always, at the back of her mind was the nagging worry that somehow old Mrs Scott would find out her guilty secret. Not that the dear old lady, now rather more friend than employer, would actually sack her, but she would hardly be overjoyed to have someone stinking of old rags in her lovely home. Not only that, but since many of the discarded bundles were heaving with lice, Kate never now felt herself to be scrupulously clean, no matter how hard she scrubbed her hands with Lifebuoy soap.

So one way and another the job did not have a great deal to commend it. Even worse, her fellow workers were the lowest of the low, their language was that of the gutter, their moral standards even lower and then also there was the ever-present problem of old Mister Cairns himself. At the very thought of him, Kate shuddered. *One thing was certain ... just let the old bugger turn his attentions to Kate Rafferty Kinnon and he'd soon enough learn some robust Irish swear-words.* Thus ran her thoughts as, with sleeves rolled back, she bent to another day at the filthy, obscene, backbreaking work.

The morning went smoothly enough up to the point where old Cairns yelled out: "Katie Kinnon. You're not working hard enough. I've had my eye on you for some time, lazy bitch that you are. Right? You got that?"

Up to the elbows in vermin-laden rags, Kate stopped at the sound of her boss's voice. And dreading any further developments, especially such as those of which her fellow workers spoke in whispers, she redoubled her efforts. But even that did not satisfy the old man.

Again he shouted: "Did ye hear me, Kinnon? I'm not paying you good money for nothing. So, just you get your lazy, fat arse into the stock room and collect another bundle of rags. At once!"

Desperately hoping that another bundle was all that she would be collecting, Kate made her way past the rows of her fellow workers, each one head bent to the task and suddenly totally engrossed.

With a sinking feeling, Kate entered the screened off area at the back of the cavern. She stared in disbelief at old man Cairns, and recoiled in horror. There he stood, his tartan breeks on the floor around his ankles. What passed for his manhood on full, obscene display. And if his intention had not already been crystal-clear he wore a slavering, lecherous leer on his wizened face.

Frozen to the spot, Kate watched events unwinding almost as if in slow motion. Then, as the filthy old man, having reached out for her, clamped a claw-like hand on her breast, the reality of her situation hit her. In an instant, galvanised into action, she tore his hand away, slapped his face hard, and ran screaming like a banshee back into the communal work area.

Kate knew, without the finality of actually being told, that her job as a rag picker was at an end. Not only had she repulsed the amorous advances of her lecherous old boss but, worse than that, she had made a fool of him in front of all his other women employees. If there was one thing the old bastard could not – and most certainly would not – endure, it was such an insult to his male ego. Other women to satisfy his lust could be had by the dozen, especially when it was a choice between a quick fumble as part of the daily grind of gainful employment or starvation for themselves and their squad of ragged and ill shod bairns.

Not that Kate, decent widow-woman she now was, had much more in the way of material wealth than her fellow employees, but one thing she did have in abundance was her innate moral sense. Add to that her wild Irish temper when roused and the old lecher had stood not a chance. By the same token, neither had Kate's job. And so here she was, standing out on the pavement in front of the rag store, thrown out at a minute's notice by the irate, purple-faced and frustrated dirty old man. She did not even have the consolation of a modicum of support from a single one of the other woman, each of whom had kept eyes down at the height of the drama.

Ah, well, such is life, thought Kate as she gathered her shawl closer around her shoulders. Although it provided but scant protection against the biting winds of February, the threadbare garment gave inestimable comfort to Kate. At the way her thoughts were running, Kate smiled.

Yes. It might not look much but this second-hand old shawl is my badge of freedom. When I think back to how Pearce used always to insist on my wearing my one and only 'best' coat to look the part of a Lady. Hmph. Some lady I turned out to be with not a halfpenny to my name. But he's gone now and if I choose to look like a shawlie-woman then that's my choice and not that of a domineering husband.

The thought cheered her and she drew herself deeper into the depths of the garment which had been her first purchase at Paddy's Market once free of the bonds of matrimony. With head now bent, as if going into battle against a cruel world, she all but collided with someone as she rounded a windswept corner into the Saltmarket.

An angry voice burst into her thoughts: "Heh. Lissen ye. Can ye no look where ye're going? Are ye daft as weel as blind?"

About to give as good as she got in this sudden war of words, Kate opened her mouth. The insults were strangled at birth when she found herself gazing into the eyes of her old pal from the early days in Candleriggs.

"I don't believe it. Betty Donovan."

Betty gave a toothless grin by way of welcome and then without further ado, she enveloped Kate in the greatest of bear-hugs. When they finally disentangled themselves, Betty was babbling away and there was nothing Kate could do to stem the torrent or even get in the occasional word on her own account.

What finally emerged was that Betty was now living in Govan; her good man was working in Fairfield's Shipyard; many of her brood were now scattered to the far corners of the Empire; Betty herself had a wee job in a place called Mac's Restaurant; and wasn't it a miracle that she should bump into Kate?

While Kate was still trying to digest at least some of this, she first focussed on the last nugget of information and said: "Mac's Restaurant indeed. My, my. And does that not sound all very grand."

Scarcely were the words out of Kate's mouth than Betty, whose ample girth had not in any way diminished over the intervening years, gave a great belly laugh and erupted into raucous laughter, all the while quivering like an enormous jelly.

When at last she could restrain herself, she wiped the tears of laughter and said: "Very grand? Is that what ye think, Kate?"

Kate nodded, still at a loss to understand, but unwilling as yet to make further comment.

Betty smiled, laid a work-red hand on her friend's arm and said: "Let me tell ye, Kate, the elegant restaurant of yer vivid imagination is otherwise known as a workman's eating place. And as for yers truly, I'm none other than the kitchen skivvy."

As they laughed together, standing there in the Saltmarket, and exchanging news of their respective families, it was as if the intervening years had never been.

"Oh, Kate, Ah'm real sorry to hear yer news. When Ah saw yer mourning bands, Ah thought they were for the Queen."

Kate gave a dismissive toss of her head. "Well, Betty, there's mourning aplenty and miles enough of black crepe across this land for her, without yours truly adding as much as a farthing's worth."

Betty nodded in ready agreement.

"True enough! What did the old biddy ever do for the likes of us?"

The two old friends were lost in thought for a moment before Kate said: "Whatever mourning I'm wearing is for Pearce and none other. So, as they say round here, ye ken noo."

Reluctant to part, the two women still stood there on the street corner, setting their worlds to right. When it was clear they could have blethered from then until Kingdom come, Kate was the first to make noises about having to get on her way. It was with a great show of reluctance and much hugging that the two finally parted company. And as Kate made her way home, it was with Betty's words still ringing in her ears: "Mind noo. Ah'm no living at the other end of the world. Just over in darkest Govan, at Langlands Road. And there's aye a cuppa tea for ye in ma wee single-end. So, be seein' ye, auld freen o mine."

On her way back home to the Candleriggs, Kate smiled happily at how her day had so suddenly got better. She was even on the point of singing when she stopped short.

Heavens above. What am I thinking of? Me, a recently bereaved widow woman. What right have I to be feeling so happy?

But no matter how she argued thus with herself, she was still aware of a wonderful elevation of her spirits. Since she had first come to Glasgow all those years ago, for the first time ever, she was free, gloriously, deliciously free. Free to go anywhere, do anything, visit friends of her own choosing, wear a coarse tweed shawl ... and all that without having to consult with and defer to any domineering, controlling snob of a husband.

Little wonder then that when she met old Shuggie at the corner of her own street, he took one look at her and said with a twinkle in his eyes: "My, and ye're lookin jist grand the day, Mistress Kinnon. Is it no wonderful what renewin an old friendship can do to revive the spirit."

Kate frowned in puzzlement.

"But Shuggie, how did you know? Don't tell me you've got the gift of second sight. I've only just left Betty Donovan."

Shuggie looked puzzled as, pushing back his flat bunnet, he scratched his head.

"I've heard Terence O'Neil called many a thing but never that."

They laughed together, but Kate felt herself blushing at the implication behind Shuggie's words. She was still smiling to herself as she entered the flat.

Even the screams of Hannah were not enough to spoil her mood. If anything, the contrast between the happiness she herself felt and the misery of what poor handicapped Hannah's life would always be, somehow underscored the sudden hope for the future which was Kate's shining star on the horizon.

Kate bustled around the flat and all the while her mind was racing. What a day it had been ... first of all she had lost her job, the hated job on which she hoped to pay off the funeral expenses; she had had a cheery wave from Terence; and not only had she renewed her friendship with Betty, but she now had an invitation to visit Govan.

It was true. Poor Pearce was scarcely cold in his grave over in the Necropolis but already her life was taking on an entirely new depth – freedom and excitement.

Chapter 3

Ever on the alert to make an honest penny with which to support her family, quite out of the blue, Kate spotted yet another opportunity for gainful employment. All over Glasgow there were little family run shops which sold, in a glorious disorganised jumble, everything from homemade toffee-balls to bundles of kindling sticks for the fire. And now, just at the corner of the next street to her home, yet another 'Jenny-aw-Things' was bursting into vibrant life. Never one to let a chance slip past her and right from day one of its opening its doors, Kate made a point of going in several times, always on the pretext of asking for items which she was pretty sure were not yet available in Mrs Henderson's wee shop. By the time a couple of weeks had passed, Kate and the owner were on the friendliest of terms because, since Kate never left the shop empty-handed, she was now considered to be a regular customer. For although Mrs Henderson as yet stocked neither floral slip-on overalls with matching elasticated mobcaps, nor chunks of puff candy, nor even sewing lapbags – all items of which Kate had seemingly had been in dire need – never-the-less Kate always bought some small article with which to show willing.

The door pinged its welcome as, for about the tenth time that week, Kate entered the Jenny-aw-Things. Looking up from where she was counting the takings at the cash drawer, the latter already equipped with its essential display of dud coins nailed round the rim, Mrs Henderson smiled. "Oh, it's yourself Mrs Kinnon. A fine bright day. And what can I do for you this morning?"

Before Kate could answer, Mrs Henderson, as if just having made up her mind to something, rushed on with: "Listen, my dear! I'm really glad you've popped in ... there's something I've been meaning to ask you. The thing is this ... I'm gradually adding to my stock, but as you yourself already know, not nearly fast enough. So here's what I wanted to suggest ..."

Leaving her ancient and hard-of-hearing father in full and rather doubtful charge of the shop, Mrs Henderson first beckoned and then drew Kate into the back kitchen. There, over a freshly brewed cup of tea and a treacle scone, the two women got down to their discussion.

"I must say, Mistress Kinnon, Kate, if I may, that over these past few weeks, you've certainly given me plenty to think about."

By now fully aware her clever marketing strategy was about to bear fruit of some kind, Kate nevertheless assumed an air of puzzlement. With a frown of concentration, she said: "Oh? And how would that be, Mistress Henderson? I'm not sure I get your drift. All I know is that in becoming a regular customer here in your wee Jenny-aw-Things, I feel that you and I are fast becoming friends."

Mrs Henderson smiled and nodded her agreement.

"Yes, friends indeed. And quite apart from your very welcome custom, I always enjoy our wee bit chat over the counter."

Kate nodded and waited for the shopkeeper to continue.

"Yes, Kate, but friendship apart, the thing is ... I have a wee business proposition for you. You see, you happened to mention in the by-going the other day that having once been a lady's maid, you're still something of a dab hand with a sewing needle."

Again Kate nodded as she waited with bated breath to hear the exact nature of what Mrs Henderson was about to propose. In the event, she did not have long to wait as the other woman's words came gushing out in an excited gabble.

"What it is ... I was wondering ... now please don't take offence ... but I thought if you'd not be averse to earning an extra half crown or so ... what about sewing some wee garments for me to sell?"

There. It was out in the open, the opportunity for which Kate had schemed, hinted at, and even prayed for. And almost as if afraid that Mrs Henderson would change her mind, Kate leant forward and shook the woman's hand by way of ready assent. Then over a fresh cup of tea, the two friends finalised the details. By the time Kate was walking on air back home, she had agreed whole-heartedly to the new venture, with firm orders already in place for a selection of work pinnies, mobcaps, lapbags, and even later on, the rather more ambitious crocheted matinee jackets, tartan waistcoats, and toorie-on-the-top Tam O'Shanters.

As they parted company at the door of the wee shop Etta Henderson had said: "Right, that's settled, Kate. And later on, if things do well, perhaps I'll even get you busy in other areas, for I hear from folk you're a wizard at the making of coconut tablet and such like dainties."

The moment Kate entered her home, she was greeted by Granny Gorbals who at once said: "Hannah's having a wee sleep in the front room. So how about I make us a cuppa before I go back across the landing for, knowing you as well as I do, it looks to me as if you're fair burstin to tell me news of some kind."

Kate laughed in delight. "Honestly Granny! It'll be a frosty Friday in Hell before I can keep any secrets from you."

In the weeks that followed, as Kate sewed far into the night, even old Granny got into the act. Declaring stoutly that, rheumatic fingers or not, she could still hold and work her magic with a crochet hook, she turned out the most enchanting little matinee jackets, bonnets, bootees, and matching ribbon-entwined mitts for new-born babies.

Then one evening, as Kate and Granny sat by the fireside in easy companionship, each plying sewing needle and crochet hook respectively, there came the biggest surprise of all.

Jenny entered the room, bringing with her a draught of cold air from the dank close below and the dimly-lit stairway beyond. Still holding Theresa in her arms, she looked at the cosy domestic scene.

"I must say, it's a right sewing-bee you've got going there, you two."

Both Kate and Granny looked up and smiled, uncertain as yet to Jenny's mood. But when still neither spoke and the silence lengthened, Jenny at last said, almost with a hint of wistfulness in her voice: "Well now, is it a private meeting? Or can anyone join in the magic circle?"

At the time of Pearce's death Jenny had been a loving and supportive daughter, despite her anger at Pearce over the disappointment of not being allowed to stay on at school and study to become a teacher, but of late Granny and Kate had each been at the mercy of Jenny's awkward, disruptive, and unreasoning moods. Kate, often wondered what had happened to the Jenny of the past. Granny and Kate exchanged meaningful glances. Whatever it was that had changed Jenny's personality so drastically, was she now in this way trying to make amends and thus be welcomed back into the bosom of the family? Determined to give her wayward, unhappy daughter the benefit of the doubt, Kate at once said: "Jenny, of course you know you're more than welcome to join us. And who knows, if your sewing pleases Mrs Henderson, you'll probably make yourself a few bawbees into the bargain."

In the event, the owner of the Jenny-aw-Things was delighted with the output of all three women. So much so, there was soon a stout brass rail stretched across the window of the wee shop and from this vantage display, there hung a selection of crocheted, knitted and hand-sewn garments. Not only that, but quite apart from a goodly collection of silver half-crowns now stored in the old china teapot on the mantelpiece there was also the very welcome bonus of a greater measure of harmony and tranquillity in the Kinnon household.

Kate's fervent prayer was that it would last.

Coming out of the Jenny-aw-Things one Saturday morning, Kate frowned. While she couldn't put her finger on exactly what the problem was, somehow she sensed that Mrs Henderson had not been her usual friendly self. Even more puzzling had been the shopkeeper's attitude when, obviously on the point of discussing something with Kate, the woman had instead turned away as she positively welcomed the arrival at the counter of Stoorie Sanny, flour-laden clothes or not. Unable to solve the mystery, if indeed not a figment of her imagination, Kate shook her head in bewilderment and made her way home.

As she came into the kitchen, she was pleasantly surprised to see that Jenny had a good fire going in the grate and wonder of wonders, she had even set out the table in readiness for their evening meal. Kate beamed in delight.

"Well, Jenny, this is a lovely surprise, I must say. And it's good that you and I seem to be getting on so much better these days." When there was no answer to the compliment, Kate went on: "It seems as if the peace and calm of our wee sewing bee is helping your nerves, Jenny. And of course the added bonus of the wage packet is always a welcome sight."

At the mention of their wee home industry, Jenny's face clouded.

"I've been meaning to ask you. Mammy ... is ... er ... well ... is Mrs Henderson still happy with our output?"

Kate nodded. "As you know, Jenny, she's paying us well and she'd hardly be doing that if she was displeased, now would she? And don't forget, she gave you a bit extra the other week for that lovely smocking you did on the baby's dress. Why, I remember how much she admired it and she even said that ..."

Kate's words trailed off. The realisation that the very same Mrs Henderson had hardly spoken a kind word to her new friend a few short hours ago, suddenly hit her like a thunderclap. As her eyes took in the cosy, well-ordered domestic scene, as prepared, uncharacteristically, by Jenny, at once everything seemed to fall into place. With narrowed eyes Kate looked at her daughter and in a low-pitched voice which spoke volumes of distrust, she said: "Right, Jenny. Just tell me this. Is there any good reason on earth as to why Mrs Henderson should not be pleased with our work?"

Jenny hung her head, fiddled with the tassels on her cardigan before finally saying: "Oh, no reason, Mammy. No reason ... I just wondered, that if ..."

Kate fixed her daughter with a steely eye.

"Jenny!"

Like a naughty schoolgirl caught out in some misdemeanour, Jenny toed patterns in the linoleum with the point of her shoe.

"Well, it's just ... that latest batch you handed in recently ... I was just wondering ... hoping ... that it was up to our usual standard."

"Jenny! Will you please stop dithering and tell me exactly what all this is about?"

This time Jenny fiddled with a lock of hair which had flopped over her forehead.

"To tell you the truth, Mammy ..."

"Please do just that, Jenny."

"Thing is, well, I wasn't feeling too good when I did those last matinee jackets."

"Nonsense, girl. You seemed perfectly well to me."

"Mammy, will you listen to me? I'd taken a wee refreshment, and ..."

Kate frowned. "A wee refreshment! Is that what you're saying? Isn't that what the local drunks, layabouts and scum of the earth euphemistically call a bucketful of cheap whisky? For God's sake, Jenny ... don't tell me you're on the Demon Drink. Please God, no!"

But whatever God in his Heaven thought about it, one thing was certain. Jenny's sullen silence was confirmation enough. Yes, it was true. Suddenly it all made sense. Jenny's dark moods, her irritability, her unreasoning temper. Kate recalled Pearce's behaviour when he had been on the drink before the death of wee Andrew. Yes, she knew at first hand how insidious was the curse of the Demon Drink.

Kate glowered at her daughter, a grown woman by now, toeing patterns in the rag rug before the fire.

"Listen, Jenny, if you were as unwell ... or let's not put too fine a point on it ... as drunk as you suggest ... I must say, you hid it well. And that only comes as a result of long practice, right?"

With these words, Kate stormed out of the house and ran to the shop. At once she was aware of a rather frosty welcome from her erstwhile friend. Determined to bring the matter into the open, Kate said: "Mrs Henderson, there's something I have to ask you ... And much as I hate to do so, for all our sakes, I must know. Was that last batch of sewing and knitting ... was everything all right?"

As if a weight had just been lifted from her mind, Mrs Henderson let out a long sigh of relief.

"Oh, Kate, I didnae like to mention it, but ..."

Kate nodded. "So there was something wrong!"

"You could say that. Oh, I admit on the surface. It all looked fine and I sold a good lot of it straight away. In fact, those wee matinee jackets that Jenny's been making, they hardly had enough time to hang on the brass rail before they were snapped up. But ..."

Kate waited with bated breath. She was amazed when instead of the catalogue of complaints she was expecting, Mrs Henderson burst out laughing. "I can see the funny side of it now, Kate. But it took a wee bit of fast talking to placate my customers. You see, the fancy crocheted edging on the sleeves and on the hem of the jackets ... well, while it all looked very decorative, it had somehow joined all the edges together and ..."

At the mental picture, even Kate had to smile. It was difficult enough to dress a wriggling babe-in-arms, but impossible to coax any bairn into a garment in which the sleeves and hems had been virtually welded together with fancy crocheted designs.

As Kate at once offered to supply another batch of work free of charge, to apologise for Jenny's poor workmanship.

The shopkeeper nodded in sympathy. "Listen, Kate, if poor Jenny was feeling ill with a sick headache, I can well realise how the mistakes were made. So please don't worry. After all, headaches like that can affect the eyesight. I should know, my old mother used to be a martyr to them. Mind you between you, me, and the shop door, I was always inclined to think that what gave my mother her headaches was that old curmudgeon of my father ... nothing ever seemed to please him, so going to bed in a darkened room with a sick headache as her only companion was maybe the only peace the poor soul ever got."

As the two women parted amicably, Kate felt an inner disgust at thus lying – or at least being rather economical with the truth – on Jenny's behalf. Even so, she was glad that her employer had been so very understanding.

At least for the moment, the wee job and the friendship were safe. And that was surely worth a white lie or two ... or was it?

Chapter 4

As Kate made her way home having finished her usual Friday evening stint of close and stair washing, the gaslit streets and vennels had their usual quota of pay-night drunks. Some reeled from one lamppost to the next; some were propped up against any convenient wall; some lay senseless in the gutter. Kate wrinkled her nose at this habitual weekend bacchanalia and tried to focus her thoughts on the more pleasant aspects of her life in Glasgow.

Yes, it would be good to get home. Now that Jenny, relieved of her sewing bee activities, and seemingly making a success of helping with the bags of puff candy at Mrs Henderson's shop, was making an effort to limit her drinking and be helpful, relations ran much more smoothly. Most Friday nights she would have the table set for Kate's late return and even a good-going fire in welcome. No doubt about it, life in the Kinnon household was much improved of late.

With this happy thought uppermost in her mind at first Kate was oblivious to the sound of her name being called from across the street.

"Haw, therr, Mistress Kinnon. Ah've goat a bone tae pick wi ye."

At the second or third call Kate peered into the gloom. A drunk man risking life and limb staggered perilously close to tramcars in his desperate attempt to reach her side. Having survived his death defying trek, he stood swaying before her.

"See you, Mistress Kinnon. Know something? Ye've just cost me a bloody fortune so ye have."

At a complete loss to understand what he was talking about Kate said: "Er ... hello there, Tommy. Now then, what's that you're trying to tell me?"

Tommy Boyde lunged towards her and they would have collided had Kate not dodged nimbly aside, causing Tommy to grab onto the nearest lamppost for support.

In an agony of indecision whether to make a bolt for freedom or not, Kate delayed a moment too long. Tommy twisted round and grabbed Kate with his free hand.

"See that?" He thrust his wide open mouth close to her. "No a fuckin tooth in ma gob, is therr?"

Kate could only stand there, with waves of nausea sweeping over her, coinciding with the gales of fumes of cheap whisky issuing from Tommy's mouth with every breath.

Finally, after several attempts to speak coherently, Tommy managed to say: "Aye, hen. A coupla days ago Ah wis the envy o aw ma pals, so Ah wis. Ah had a full set o dentures, tap and bottom, great gnashers. Goat them frae the Glesca Dentorium. Happy tae be payin them up at hauf-a-croon a week fur the next coupla years."

Still unsure where this garbled tale was heading, Kate could only stand and listen in mounting trepidation.

"Thon gnashers – really changed ma life, worth every penny. E'en ma auld woman, she'd taen a second notion fur me. Talk aboot a second honeymoon! But noo, and aw thanks tae ye, Ah'm back tae being a gumsy – no wan fuckin tooth left."

He paused for breath.

"It was yon bloody puff candy ye make – mair like cahoutchy – it stuck tae ma dentures like glue. Ah tried tae pull them free. So whit happened? Ma dentures went fleeing oot ma mooth and afore Ah could catch ontae them they were doon the nearest stank."

The week after the puff-candy disaster and the resulting confrontation with the inebriated Tommy Boyde, Kate was feeling decidedly low in spirits. She couldn't afford to reimburse Tommy for his loss and Terence when she told him had thought it a huge joke. Always very attuned to Kate's moods, Granny Gorbals suggested that Kate meet up with a friend of hers and attend a forthcoming lantern lecture. The riveting topic was to be 'The Demon Drink' followed by 'the cup that cheers but not inebriates' and a bun at the interval, then a promised light-hearted look at 'Humours of the Kirk in the Olden Days'.

Once seated on a hard bench in the draughty hall, Kate and Jumble Jean, so called from her expertise at jumble sales, settled themselves to the evening of free entertainment. There was much declaiming of the Demon Drink from the invited speaker up on the platform, followed by lurid pictures of the drunkard's haggard, pitiful wife, his hovel of a family home, and their destitute children one and all bare-foot, ragged, and starving.

The captive audience, by now thirsting for the promised cup of tea, were getting a bit restive, there was much rustling of sweetie pokes and shuffling of booted feet on the wooden floor. Finally relating to the mood of his audience, the speaker cast about desperately for another tack with which to revive their so obviously flagging interest. He cleared his throat, then fixing a beady eye on one particularly inattentive old man who by now was muttering obscenities under his breath – about having spent a better night 'wi the fuckin toothache' – the speaker announced in what he thought were tones of great joy: "So, as we already know from those wonderful lantern slides – and, of course, my talk to you on the subject – much work has been done over the years to help beleaguered families enmeshed in the horrors brought on by the Demon Drink. Strangely enough, one of its most powerful weapons in our armoury has been – wait for it – a poem! Yes! Ladies and gentlemen, a poem! And written by a registrar of Govan a wonderful caring human being who came to be known as

The Laureate of the Temperance Movement.

"The emotive words of 'The Drunkard's Ragged Wean' were inspired when James P Crawford, bored –"

At this point Jumble Jean dug Kate in the ribs and whispered: "Bored out of his skull by a dull as ditchwater minister like this one."

The speaker glared round the audience with a final fishlike stare at Kate.

"– and bored by a dull sermon, was on the point of disgracing himself by nodding off to sleep right there in that Glasgow church. In an effort to keep himself awake, James slunk further down on to the pew and then, hopefully out of view of the minister still rambling on, James Crawford took out a stub of pencil and started writing what amazingly would become a world-famous poem.

"And that, my friends, is a good point at which to break for tea … while leaving the door open, as it were, to entertain you later with some rather amusing stories of 'Humours of the Kirk in the Olden Days.'"

As they savoured the longed for cup of tea and munched happily at their Paris buns, Kate and Jumble Jean chatted.

"Aye" said Kate, "I don't know about the rest of all thon stuff he was telling us, but the speaker got at least one thing right. He's spot on about that famous poem. In fact, they do say that when it was first published in the 1880's in the 'Crystal Fount' it ran to something like thirty-three thousand copies."

Martha laughed. "Listen, Kate, seems to me you know more about it than that eejit of a guest speaker. Mibbe you should be giving the second half of the lecture … at least that way, we might just get a real belly laugh. If it's left to auld droopy drawers up therr, mibbe we'll all end up writing poetry just to keep oorsels awake."

Kate giggled. "Uch well! Surely to goodness if he's advertised it as 'The Humours of the Kirk' it stands to reason there must be a wee bit of light relief in it somewhere. Anyway, here's hoping."

The tea urn, tin mugs, and assorted other accoutrements cleared away in a riot of sound and activity, the self-important speaker, who doubtless had had more than his fair share of all the available buns and cakes, again got to his feet. He cleared his throat and in a good imitation of a strict disciplinarian Dominie, his gaze swept round the hall until his steely glare had quelled even the most garrulous of the unruly mob.

"The Humours of the Kirk ... yes, an unusual topic, I do agree. Now then, where to start?"

Jumble Jean's *sotto voce* comment about starting by going home earned her a murderous look.

Perhaps as a last ditch effort to redeem his reputation, the speaker got into his subject with the zeal of an avenging angel. In a highly dramatic way he told amusing stories about Church Beadles who got the better of their Ministers; Ministers who got the last word with their recalcitrant Beadles, and ordinary Kirk members such as wee wifies with waspish tongues, who got the better of both of them. Not to mention those sneaky members of every congregation who either took money out of the velvet collection bag or plate, or else surreptitiously deposited a handful of buttons or even the infamous Dutch coins known as doits.

He told of one particular Beadle who with his pawky, snide, sense of humour got the better of many a pompous young Minister. Such as the time when asked by the new Minister as to what passage of the sermon had pleased him the most, had replied: "Weel, Meenister, if Ah'm being honest ... it was your eventual passage frae the pulpit back to the vestry I liked best."

Later, after the evening's entertainment was over and Kate was home, Granny was desperate to hear more of the amusing stories which had survived over the long years of the Kirk's history.

"Well, Granny, we'd be here all night if I went through them all. And anyway, Jumble Jean has invited the pair of us round to her house one evening for a wee blether and a cup of tea and to go over the stories at our leisure."

Chapter 5

As Kate bustled about her kitchen making a clootie dumplin for a special teatime treat, she hummed softly to herself.

Certainly Jenny, although unemployed again except for a one day a week cleaning job after having given up on the sewing and candy making venture, hardly lifted a finger to help with the household chores. She was increasingly truculent and bad tempered about her station in life, blaming Kate for allowing Pearce to send her to work in the Mill instead of letting her stay on at school eventually to become a teacher. With Pearce dead the bitter animosity over this had transferred itself to Kate and acrimonious exchanges between them were increasingly frequent.

Even so, now that Kate had more or less resigned herself to the situation, and tried not to respond to Jenny's emotional outbursts, a more peaceful atmosphere had of late reigned in the Kinnon home.

In addition, and secretly, Kate attributed the cease-fire to the handsome Terence O'Neil who, with his Irish charm, and a cheeky joke for every occasion, had taken to dropping in unannounced at the flat. His feeble excuse each time was that he had found yet another slim volume of poetry for Kate. But since Jenny too always seemed in a much better humour both during and after his visits, Kate had seen no earthly reason to discourage him in any way from his frequent appearances.

Terence started off the evening well for Kate by announcing that friends of his worked in the city sanitary department and for a 'small consideration' had lifted the stank Tommy's dentures had vanished into and investigated the trap below. Since there had been no storm water to flush the stank the dentures were still there and had been restored to their delighted owner.

In the course of the evening's laughter-filled teatime Terence announced that his church was holding a soiree the coming Saturday evening and asked Kate to go with him.

"Oh, Terence, I'd love to. But it's not yet a full three months since Pearce died. What would people say? Me, a widow woman still in deep mourning – a year and a day it is – out at a public function and not even decently with another woman, but with a man."

Terence laughed. "Who gives a damn what people think? It's nobody's business but ours. However, if you're set on following the convention to the letter, I'll not press you. But it would be good fun."

At the look of disappointment on Terence's face, Kate blurted out: "Why don't you take Jenny?"

"I'm old enough to be her father," Terence protested.

Jenny and Kate both laughed and the subject was more or less dropped.

The rest of the evening passed pleasantly enough, but when Terence was leaving it was Jenny who went with him to the door, there to bid him good-night.

When she came back into the room, it was a rosy-cheeked, dreamy-eyed Jenny who sat down at the kitchen table. First of all she examined her fingernails, then fiddled with the bobbles of table's chenille cover. Finally, she cleared her throat.

"Just thought you'd like to know, Mammy ... Terence has invited me as his partner to his Church's soiree on Saturday."

The words were spoken like a challenge.

"Hmph," Kate said. "Well, if he's asked you out, my girl, it's not for want of those awful hints you threw at the poor man all evening. You should be ashamed of yourself."

As if accepting these comments as some sort of compliment, Jenny preened and giggled coyly.

"Listen Mother, he's been round here often enough, so I just knew he was dying to ask me to walk out with him, but he was just too shy. Anyway, I know I can get any man I want, but in his case, it just took a little more persuasion."

Kate bit at her lower lip, as if to hold back the words she knew would spew forth and cause trouble between them.

Finally, when she could keep silent not a minute longer, she said: "You can get any man you want, Jenny? Oh, I know that to be true. What with your track record and a bastard child to show for your efforts out of wedlock, I'd be the first to agree with you there."

Jenny gasped, but before she could reply, Kate rushed on: "Honest to God, Jenny. With your morals, or rather the lack of them, you're little short of the lowest woman of the streets. Why would you think a decent man would be interested in the likes of you ... Terence is far too good for you. And, my lady, just one thing you're forgetting, he is my friend. All these months he's been coming round here to see me ... not a little tramp like you."

With the finish of this onslaught, Jenny erupted into hysterical laughter. Then standing arms akimbo, she shouted: "Handsome or not, the dashing Terence is like all men ... he's after only one thing! You've told me that often enough in the past. If you think a dried-up old widow like you could possibly satisfy his needs, then you'd better think again. Your friend indeed ... don't make me laugh."

Kate raised a shaking hand and it took every drop of willpower for her not to slap it, hard, against her daughter's cheek. As Kate lowered her hand, she looked at it as if in a dream. Then almost without volition, she sat down on the nearest chair.

As the two women stared at each other, the hate-filled silence lengthening between them, finally Kate said: "You know, if it weren't for the sake of wee Theresa, I'd make you pack your bags and leave this very night."

Jenny tossed her head disdainfully.

"Oh, don't you worry on that score, Mammy. I'll be leaving, that's for sure. But not tonight. I'll go when it bloody suits me. Once I've got Terence, or any other man for that matter, to look after us, wee Theresa and I will clear off out this rat-hole and go as far away from you as we can get."

Kate put her head in her hands.

Seeing this, Jenny, always one to press home her advantage, said: "Anyway, whatever you say, I'll be going out with Terry and –"

Kate's head jerked up at this. "Terry! Oh, so it's Terry now, is it. Not even his Sunday name."

"Uch, give it a rest Mammy. I think we've said all we need for now. And at least one thing's sure … we both know exactly where we stand, don't we?"

As Jenny slammed her way out of the room, Kate was left with her own thoughts.

Refusing to allow her vivid imagination to dwell on the image of her daughter, her wayward daughter, dancing and held close in the arms of Kate's own secretly-beloved, handsome Terence, Kate suddenly dredged up a happier scenario.

Surely I haven't imagined all those shared, secret glances between us. I'm sure Terence has feelings for me. Oh, wait a minute. I've got it. Oh, the darling. The clever, amazing, debonair, wonderful man. I know what he's doing. He does know he cannot hope to court me yet awhile. But this way, by hinting to me of his love with the treasured gifts of poetry volumes, and with Jenny living here and being here when he calls, the stage is set. It means he can come and go freely without causing any undue gossip. Yes. That's the answer, I'm sure. It's just that Jenny is desperate for any man and is determined to throw her cap at him. Still, as long as Terence and I both know where we stand ... and there is a definite silent bond of communication between us ... it will all work out. Yes. He's a clever one, my own darling Terence.

On the Saturday evening of the soiree, Jenny hummed happily as she prepared for the outing.

"When do you expect Terence to call for you?" Kate said, finally.

"Oh, he's not coming here for me. I'll meet him at the church. He's not ever going to be here again. I'm sure he'll find someplace nice for us to meet in future."

Jenny gave a final pat to her hair standing at the room door. "Don't bother waiting up for me."

"The soiree finishes at half-past-ten," Kate said.

Jenny laughed. "Yes ... it does ... but I don't expect the evening to end then. Good night, Mammy."

For the whole week following the soiree Kate expected Terence to call each evening, but in vain. When Saturday came round again Jenny announced she would be out that evening, but Kate didn't ask who she would be with and Jenny didn't offer a name.

Kate spend a miserable evening, alone except for Hannah and Theresa.

Am I wrong and Terence is really enamoured of Jenny? Kate thought, *I couldn't stand that. What then? God help me she's my own daughter, but I wouldn't inflict her on my worst enemy, far less on my darling Terence.*

The following Friday, Jenny said she would be out for the evening again without giving Kate any details. Shortly after Jenny left the flat Kate heard a knock on her door.

"Terence! Come in. Jenny's out I'm afraid."

"I know. I've been outside across the street these last four nights waiting, hoping, she would go out. It's you I want to see, to talk to, not her."

"You took her to the soiree –"

"Damn it, woman, because you suggested it! I told both of you, I'm old enough to be her father. Old enough to have seen the likes of her before. Not old enough or glaikit enough to fall into her trap."

"But you always come when she's here …"

"Not always if you think back. In any case she lives here, doesn't she?"

"But Jenny says …"

"To hell with what Jenny says. Damn it, woman, if you weren't the decent woman you are I'd have asked you leave that old bastard, Pearce, and come live with me."

Kate looked open mouthed at Terrence. "You really mean that?"

"I'll wait out your year and a day's widow weeds since you're determined to be respectable, but I'll want your answer then. From now on, I'll not be calling round if Jenny's in the house."

When Jenny returned she looked surprised to find her mother still up, and even more surprised when Kate said: "Did you have a good evening? Sit a spell. I'll make some tea and you can tell me all about it."

Warily, Jenny sat opposite Kate at the kitchen table.

"You're all right then about me and Terry going out together?"

"I'm a bit surprised to smell whisky on your breath. Terence isn't much of a drinker and I didn't think he'd take you out drinking."

"You know nothing about him! He's a real man, not the namby-pamby creature of your soft-headed imagination. I'll nail

40

him and we'll leave you here to cry about him."

"You've been seeing him then?"

"What do you think we were doing that Saturday after the soiree? I didn't wander round sucking my thumb till two in the morning. Yes, I'm seeing him. Last Saturday and again tonight. Where did you think I've been?"

"Oh, I just wondered. Seeing as how Terence was here with me as soon as you turned the corner out of sight."

Jenny's sudden jump out of her chair almost toppled the table. With an oath she ran out of the kitchen and the outer door slammed shut behind her.

Next morning when Kate rose she peeped into the front room to check on Theresa and Hannah. Jenny was lying on the bed fully clothed and the room stank of cheap whisky. Kate crept over the window to open it.

As she did so Jenny stirred, groaned and said: "I hope you're happy now! You've managed to ruin my chance again. And don't go on about the booze. Surely I'm allowed some small pleasures."

Kate ignored the jibe and life in the Kinnon house reverted to long periods of silence interspersed with angry quarrels.

Chapter 6

Another cool morning and still smarting from one more row with Jenny, Kate made her way over to her wee job at Mrs Scott's home. At least there, she knew she would get not only a kind word but a sympathetic ear and a lovely cup of tea with her employer before starting to clean the flat. With this thought in mind, Kate felt her spirits rise and she quickened her steps in anticipation of a bit of normal conversation in stark contrast to the fishwife bawling and shouting of earlier that morning.

As was her usual practice, Kate put her key in the lock and prepared to call a welcoming, "hello!" to Mrs Scott. But for some reason, and despite turning the key this way and that, it just would not budge. Then, in desperation and much as she hated to disturb the frail old woman by bringing her from her bedroom, Kate was nevertheless compelled to beat a tattoo on the brass lion's head.

Resigning herself to a bit of a wait in allowing Mrs Scott time to shuffle her way along the hall, Kate was astounded when the door was opened almost on the very last beat of the tattoo. Kate's eyebrows shot up when the door widened further to reveal a stranger, a woman who with a pained expression on her haughty face, looked down her nose and said: "Yes? what do you want, my good woman?"

Kate felt the blood rush to her cheeks at being so addressed. She had dealt with enough so-called gentry in the course of her life to know when she was being talked down to. A member of the despised, underpaid working-class she might be, but Kate had her pride. Also, she knew well that over the years Mrs Scott had come to rely not only on Kate's housekeeping skills, but perhaps even more, on her honesty, compassion, and ongoing friendship.

So, keeping her Irish temper well in check, Kate gave a bright smile and in her most posh voice, said: "The fact of the matter is that I don't want a single thing from you, Ma'am ... whoever you might be. But thank you kindly for asking. It's Mistress Scott I've come to see."

At these words and the way in which they had been delivered, the stranger flushed angrily. She opened her mouth to reply, but a weak voice wavering from the depths of the flat stopped her in her tracks.

This was invitation enough for Kate to push her way past and head towards Mrs Scott's bedroom. On seeing Kate, the old woman raised her head and smiled in greeting. But even this feeble effort clearly sapped her strength and it was left to the stranger, who had now joined them, to take charge of the situation. Kate, always very astute in such matters, soon realised the officious stranger was none other than the old woman's niece and she had obviously crawled out of the woodwork at the very hint of a last will and testament.

When, almost in mid-sentence, Mrs Scott dozed off again, Miss Kemp nodded briskly towards the hallway and motioned Kate to follow her. There in the dim hallway already bereft of its oil paintings, silver, and brass ornaments, the cold-hearted woman gave Kate the news which left her senses reeling. Kate felt like some idiot child, standing there with mouth agape as she struggled to take in all that was being said.

The woman frowned at Kate. "I've said it once, but I'll say it again. It's clear that my aunt, my dear Aunt Scottie, is, well, anyone can see the poor old girl is dying. I spotted it right away when I arrived here on Sunday. And she's in her dotage. She's been drivelling on about changing her will. Wants to leave her money, her flat, indeed all her valuables to some street urchin. I can tell you, there's nobody Irish in our family and most certainly no-one called Theresa. So, I've decided ..."

Much of the rest of what the woman said was lost on Kate. She came out of her nightmarish daze in time to hear the redoubtable Miss Kemp say: "So I'm taking dear Aunt Scottie to Dunoon. The poor soul can end her days in comfort at my estate there. Not, of course, that I have any need of her paintings or her other bits and pieces, but I've packed them up anyway. She'll feel better with some of her own things around her."

Kate had her own reservations as to how good her old friend would feel when at the mercy of this heartless bitch on some God-forsaken estate in Argyll. But Kate was glad she had kept not only her own counsel but her dignity to the last when she heard the venom-dripped words thrown at her.

"So, as of now, my good woman, I am dispensing with your services. Yes, this very minute. Not a minute longer do you need to stay here in my Aunt's house. So, on your way with you. We'll not trouble you further."

With these words she ushered Kate to the door. Then came her parting shot: "And if my Aunt promised you any keepsakes, forget it. Her words were the ramblings of a senile old woman."

Kate opened her mouth to reply, but the shrew seemed determined to have the last word. "So such a promise no longer holds. Such arrangements were simply the product of her deranged mind. So, be off with you."

As Kate made her way along the road, the sights, sounds, and smells of the Glasgow streets might never have existed for all the notice that Kate afforded them. Her head was reeling with the mental anguish of all that she had been told and she was unsure what to do next. One thing was certain ... there would be no going back home in her present state, she could no more face up to Granny Gorbals' intuitive questioning than fly in the air. She frowned as she wondered what on earth to do with the rest of her morning. Yes, she would need to start looking for another wee job to fill in the empty days left from Mrs Scott's timetable. She would definitely need to look out for something else, but not today and not in her present state of mind. Anyway, where on God's earth would she start?

Then, thinking she had perhaps seen enough of the gentry for one day, she pressed on with head lowered. But as her thoughts took her ever further down this tortuous mental path, she again raised her head as if to take stock of her situation. She was in time to see a horse-drawn tramcar trundling down the street towards her. An inner voice deep in her subconscious seemed to be saying to her: *Get on that tram car now. Yes, now! And go over to Govan to see Betty.*

She'd visited Betty in response to her invitation and she knew this tram would take her to connect with the new-fangled steam tramcar that ran down the south side of the river to Govan Road, and it was a short walk through Elder Park to Betty's home on Langlands Road.

As Kate sat in the steam powered tram rumbling along, her mind went back to her first visit to Betty ...

The great day had dawned at last. Granny Gorbals would look after Hannah and wee Theresa, leaving Kate free of any encumbrance. Good old Granny entering into the spirit of the event had made a batch of her famous soda bread, and even a few treacle scones, all of which she had wrapped in a cloth, in readiness for Kate to take as the customary 'wee mindin' to her friend Betty.

Once settled on the slatted wooden seat of the open upper deck on this – her first ever – ride on a steam tramcar, Kate gazed out at the passing scene. She raised her head to find the tram conductor glaring down at her. Then with his hand poised over the ticket punch in readiness, he said: "Listen, Missus, Ur ye deef or somethin? Fur aboot the hundredth time ... whaur ur ye goin?"

As one coming out of a dream, Kate gazed at the uniformed man standing before her.

Kate blushed painfully and fumbled in her purse for the necessary coppers. Having handed over her money, which was accepted with very bad grace, Kate then hesitantly asked if he would be kind enough to advise her when she got to her stop, since she was new to the Govan area.

The man shoved back his uniform cap with his thumb, puffed out his cheeks. "God help us. Noo ye're wantin' a conducted tour o glorious Govan. Whit next? Weel, Ah'll try tae mind that yer ladyship's wantin' escorted aff at Elder Park. But Ah cannae promise. Like as no Ah'll be busy."

He punched the ticket with unnecessary force and thrust it into Kate's hand.

In the event, it was not the conductor who told Kate the exact stopping place for her onward journey. As they were passing the railyard at Govan Cross, a workman jumped aboard and sat in the seat just across from her. Catching her look as he lit up and began puffing away contentedly at an old clay pipe, he said: "Aye, Missus. Ma wife's the same as ye. She aye gies me a dirty look when Ah start puffin away, as she puts it, like the 'Nellie Dean' sailin' doon the Clyde tae Rothesay on a Ferr Saturday."

Even the very mention of the holiday town of Rothesay was enough to fill Kate's eyes with tears as she instantly recalled the tragedy of her one and only family holiday 'doon the watter'.

The elderly man pushed back the rim of his bunnet with an oil-stained finger, and with a frown said: "Here, lissen, Missus, if ma auld clay pipe worries ye aw that much, nae problem, hen. Ah'll move tae the ither end of the tram. For that matter, Ah could even tamp it oot, Ah suppose."

Kate dabbed at her eyes, and took a deep breath. "No, no, sir. Don't do any of that on my account. The fault's entirely mine. And believe me, it has nothing whatever to do with your pipe. It was the mention of Rothesay. You see, that was when ... it was ... well, one of my daughters drowned there, a lovely wee girl and the apple of her father's eye. Aye, drowned, on a lovely calm summer's day. Drowned in of all places the so-called Sweet Rothesay Bay. Not so sweet for me or my family, I can tell you."

"Aw, hen. That was a real sin, so it was. Mind you, it's one hell of a life, is it no? God help me ... if there's one thing Ah ken aboot, it's drownin, whether it's in Bonnie Rothesay Bay or just roonaboot Govan's Linthouse, when a brand new boat capsizes, it's aye the same end result ... heartbreak for families. Yon bloody boat. Three strapping sons Ah lost on that ill-fated apology for a Clyde-built ship."

Kate nodded. "Believe me, sir, I know exactly what you're talking about. That was the Daphne. I was there ... at that very launch ... I witnessed it. The pipe-bands, the music, the laughter, the bunting, the excitement, and the bairns all in high glee ... and then ... then. ... that terrible silence ..."

Kate's travelling companion took the pipe from his mouth, thought for a moment, then said: "Aye, lass. That was the silence of death. Then, as you know, all hell broke loose."

The elderly gentleman made sure that Kate got off at her right stop. As she alighted, and before heading into Elder Park, she gave a wave of her hand and a smile to her erstwhile companion. Her last view of him was through a haze of smoke from his clay pipe as the tram went screeching on its way along Govan Road.

For some reason, Kate's talk with the old man had strengthened her resolve – life went on. Yes, she would make a success of the rest of her life; she would work her fingers to the bone, if necessary to provide for her family; she would use to full advantage whatever resources she had or which came her way over time. True, nobody on planet earth could ever legislate for the trials and tribulations which Fate, or an all seeing God, might or might not bestow but of one thing she was sure. No man would ever again rule her life. She was, and would continue to be, her own person. Quite how, as yet, Terence O'Neil fitted this scenario, did not concern her.

Today is good, tomorrow will be even better. As for the past ... it's another country, once visited and now, best forgotten ...

Kate's reverie was interrupted by the conductor of the tramcar on her second steam-powered journey touching her shoulder.

So much for wishful dreaming, she thought. *Oh well, 'the best laid schemes o mice and men gang aft aglee and lee us nocht but grief and pain for promised joy.'*

"This is the Elder Park," the conductor said. "Ye said ye wanted aff there."

So a short time later she was at Betty's home being given a rapturous welcome.

Quick to notice the look of surprise on Betty's face, Kate at once launched into a garbled tale to account for her unexpected arrival on Betty's doorstep.

Betty waved aside the barrage of words. Then in reply to Betty's inquiry, Kate hurried on: "Oh, how am I, did you say? I'm fine thanks, Betty, just fine. In fact, never been better."

Her friend took one look at Kate's face and then as though talking to a not-very-bright bairn, Betty wagged an admonitory finger and said: "Right, now! Suppose we try all that again, old pal. It may have escaped yer notice ower the years, but whatever ye think, Ah'm no daft! And if ye're just fine, as ye put it, then what ye see before ye, is a kilted Highlander ... kilt, skean dhu, bagpipes an' all."

At this mental image of the well-upholstered Betty in the guise of a bagpipe-playing kiltie, the two friends erupted into hysterical laughter. They went on giggling to the point where they were holding on to each other for support.

Finally, when she could stand it no longer, Kate pulled away and, holding on to the stitch in her side, said: "Don't know about you, Betty, but that good old giggle has done me more good than any dose of Syrup of Figs or even a gutful of Gregory's mixture."

Again Betty laughed.

"While ye're at it, why dinnae ye mention Dr Jamieson's Pink Pills for Pale People. Anyway, whatever of that, fine well Ah know ye were feeling like hell warmed up when ye walked in here. So, jist what exactly is going on? Ur ye grieving sore ower yer good man's death? Is that it? Or is it another barney of a row with yon Jenny daughter of yers? It disnae matter a tuppeny damn, but anything that upsets ye like that, well, surely ye know ye can tell me."

The sorry tale was soon told. In the silence that followed, both women were deep in thought, frowning ferociously. At last, and after several cups of strong tea, Betty folded her arms and, assuming an air of authority, said: "Right, hen. The way I see it … and first things first … ye're needin a job o some kind. And pretty damn quick at that. So, here's what we dae."

Later that very same week, Kate was elbow deep in soapy water, dirty dishes, and acres of metal pots the size and weight of witch's cauldrons. The heat in the kitchen, between the cooking, the steam from the soup pots, and the waves of warmth issuing from the massive coal-fired range, was a tangible presence. It enveloped them all: Kate, Betty, Alec the cook, and, no respecter of persons, even the irascible Auld Mac himself. As the hour of noon approached, the level of activity seemed to keep pace with not only the rising temperature but also the mounting excitement in the kitchen.

Alec, ladle in hand, gave the black pot a stir, sniffed the aroma and said: "Aye, girls, a good pot of Scotch broth, now ready and waiting for those hungry lads, the minute their dinner hour starts."

Kate nodded. Still new to the job, she had already formed a high opinion of the quality of Alec's soup.

Quite apart from the shipyard workers, long before the hour of noon, women in their ragged shawls, and children, all knees and elbows in their dark Parish jerseys, would push their way forward in the carrying-out trade queue, each one pressing for a sniff of the steaming brew. Alec, or on occasion Auld Mac, would preside over the cauldron, and with each stir, each tuppenny-worth poured into a waiting, chipped enamel jug, those further back in the line would be in an agony of indecision. Might the day's supply of carrying-out soup run out before it was their turn; or, on the other hand, was it better to hang back in the hope that they would get the last serving with the rich scrapings of any vegetables still sticking to the bottom of the pot?

Kate was also aware that with the sound of the work's hooter at noon, all hell would be let loose.

The moment the yard gates at Fairfield's Shipyard opened to signal release from their morning's labours, the hordes of workers – be they platers, fitters, carpenters, painters, caulkers, or hauders-on – each would come running across Govan Road, defying death and injury from the steam tramcar in a bid to be first at Auld Mac's for a quick, satisfying, but affordable hot dinner.

Other sprinters who were lucky enough to live in any one of the local tenements would also belt along the road at high speed, then, taking the steps three at a time, be seated at the kitchen table in a matter of minutes – in many cases to sample Auld Mac's dinner carried home from the takeout queue.

But for those workers from across the Clyde at Partick, or from the Gorbals, or Saltmarket, or even like Kate, from the Candleriggs, for them it would be a case of every man for himself to secure a seat at the long lino-topped tables at Auld Mac's in Elder Street.

Betty would rush to the tables to take the first orders. Kate would wipe her soapy hands and stand beside Alec at the ready to carry out to the waiting men their bowls of steaming broth.

As Kate watched the hungry workmen getting tucked into the

meal, real comfort food to fill empty bellies on a cold day, she smiled contentedly to herself: *Thank God Betty managed to get me this wee job. It helps me to keep body and soul together. And even with tramcar fare twice a day, it still leaves me with a penny or two to call my own. Yes! Suddenly life is good.*

On that happy thought, she returned to the kitchen with a pile of dirty dishes.

Chapter 7

Kate sank into her chair in front of an unlit fire. As she looked at the drab sight, she frowned, remembering better days before the row with Jenny about Terence.

Honestly. As if Jenny could not have banked it up before she went out. Even a couple of those new fangled briquette things tossed into the embers would at least have kept it going.

Abandoning these thoughts, she half rose from her chair. But after today's extra hard day of toiling at Mac's Workman's Restaurant with the added supper shift for men working overtime and a ride home in two over-crowded, rattling tramcars redolent with the oil fumes from the worker's overalls, even the slightest effort was beyond her. So, after a quick check on Hannah and Theresa asleep in the front room, resigning herself the reality of her cheerless homecoming, she leant back against the cushion. Chilled to the bone she might be, but even so, having closed her eyes, in no time, she was drifting off to sleep. It was the rattle of the letterbox which brought her to instant wakefulness. At once her brain was racing: *There's no posties at this time of night. And nobody else ever makes a racket like that. Hmph. Probably some of that wild tribe of bairns from the next close. Uch. To hell. Leave them to it. They'll soon tire of that stupid game.*

Having thus convinced herself, Kate again settled to her snooze. It was not to be. There came another rat-a-tat, even louder than the first onslaught on her much-prized, good, brass letterbox. *Well, she was damned if she would keep polishing it faithfully*

*every day for the doubtful pleasure of having a welter of sticky
fingers prints bespattered all over it.*

By now, with face aflame and temper fuelling strength to her
aching limbs, she got to her feet.

*Ignore them nothing. High time I gave those weans the sharp
end of my tongue. Not much to ask ... a bit of peace and quiet after
a hard day's work.* So ran her thoughts as she all but pulled the
door from its hinges when she yanked it open.

The sight that met her eyes stemmed a flow of angry words in
mid-sentence.

As she stood there, mouth agape, it was as if time had not just
stopped, but gone hurtling backwards, and now she was in fact
looking at a ghost from the far-distant past. But no ethereal entity
this, as Kate soon discovered when with a whoop of delight, he
swept her up into his powerful, all embracing arms. If Kate had
been speechless before, by now she was breathless, as she all the
while fought to get enough air into her lungs to breathe his beloved
name. As they stood there, locked in a timeless embrace, Kate felt
that all her prayers had finally been answered. Perhaps there was a
God in His Heaven after all ... a God, who, having looked down
on Kate Kinnon's ongoing struggle for survival in the battle of life,
had decided that a lift to her heart at least once every decade or so
would neither be out of order, nor even in any danger of spoiling
her.

At last freed from the bear-hug, Kate leant her head back,
gazed in love, wonder and joy before finally whispering in a voice
muffled by emotion: "Danny! Is it really you ... my very own
Danny Boy?"

He grinned down at her and with a saucy wink said: "Well, if
it's not your own Danny Boy ... would you mind telling me this
... are you in the habit of cuddling with wild abandon every
strange man who has the temerity to rattle your precious
letterbox?"

Kate chortled with such unbridled laughter as she had not

known in years. When it was clear that not only could she have gone on laughing but that a note of hysteria was already creeping in, Danny hurried to say: "Right now, mother o' mine ... am I to be kept out here on the doorstep, like an abandoned parcel, for the duration of my visit?"

His words, albeit spoken in jest, were enough to galvanise Kate into action. Danny's feet scarcely touched the ground as he was bustled into the kitchen. And having deposited his jacket on the nearest chair, one look at the dead fire was enough to tell him of his mother's exhaustion, despair and lack of human comfort. So, without a word, and, Kate wondered, if perhaps also to mask his own emotion, Danny set about rekindling the fire. In the shortest time, by dint of throwing some sugar on the coals and holding a newspaper against the frame of the range as he had seen Mammy herself do so many times in years past, he had managed to get a cheery glow. And once settled in front of the now comfortable hearth, he grinned across at her. On the point of speaking, he bit back the words when Kate got there first.

"So, here we are, Danny Boy. I can't tell you how wonderful it is to see you. And after all this time. You know, I always kept hoping, aye and praying, praying desperately that one day you would return."

He nodded, leant over and placed a hand on his mother's arm. "The truth is, Mammy, I've been wanting to come back for years now. But as you know, I vowed never again to enter this house while Dadda was here. But when I heard that he was seriously ill and likely be so be some time – a friend in a pub mentioned it to me just before my ship last sailed ... that was when I decided ..."

Kate nodded encouragement for her son to go on.

"Yes, I made up my mind that the very next time my ship would dock in Glasgow ... the least I could was to come back to the family home. And if possible, perhaps make my peace with the old man."

"Oh, Danny son. That must have been in January. Your Dadda

was ill. But he's dead and buried. And lying over in the Necropolis these past months."

Danny bent his head and examined his fingernails. At last, he cleared his throat. "I'm no hypocrite Mammy, so I'll make no noises of regret. And while I would certainly have tried to make my peace with him – had he still been in the land of the living – that was maybe more for my benefit than for his. I'll not speak ill of the dead, regardless of how I was treated by him. But had I known he was in fact no longer with us, there's one thing certain sure. I'd have jumped ship, moved heaven and earth, in fact, done anything in my power to get back home to you. What I'm trying to say is that you and I would have been reunited long before now."

Tears were by now rolling down Kate's cheeks and it was a moment before she could trust herself to speak.

"You always were a good boy Danny. You've always had the welfare of the family at the forefront of your heart. Look how you gave me that money from his kin in Ireland, yon time. Money which all went on Dadda's funeral expenses although he wouldn't let me spend a penny of it on him or the family while he lived. Let's not rake up the past – the bitter past."

Danny nodded and in all solemnity said: "I couldn't agree more, Mammy. Mind you, out in the outside world, I'm maybe not as good as you seem to think. But that's another story, so as the saying goes, we'll let that flea stick to the wall for the moment anyway. But back to family matters, Mammy. Just think, think how very different our lives could have been if only ..."

Kate nodded. "If only ... the two saddest words in the entire language ... But the past is another country ... so let's leave it now and we'll never visit it again."

On that note, they sealed their agreement with a couple of tots of the water of life. But no cheap medicinal bottle this, rather the best malt whisky from a bottle Danny produced from his seabag. As they enjoyed the unexpected treat, not only of the whisky but of the luxury of their impromptu reunion, they sat in companionable silence, both alone with their thoughts. The only sound in the room was the rhythmic ticking of the wag-at-the-wall, the clatter of a sound from poor handicapped Hannah in the front room as she called out in her usual troubled sleep.

Danny cleared his throat.

"Mammy, I've done well at sea and I've just taken a job with a company that sails out of Glasgow, so I'll be here more often. I'm thinking of taking a wee single-end near the docks –"

"You don't need to do that. You can sleep over here when you're in Glasgow."

"Well, no, Mammy, I think a wee single-end would be best … the fact is –"

He was interrupted by the noise of a door crashing shut and the sound of something falling. This cacophony was followed by a stream of oaths as a dishevelled figure staggered into the living room and then stood swaying before them.

Kate said not a word but the tightening of her lips to form a hard, straight line spoke volumes.

"Well, well! If this isnae real cosy!" Jenny said. "My Mammy and a strange man at the fireside gettin tore intae a bloody great bottle o whisky. Hmph. All right for some. Ah must say."

Kate flushed, then more in sorrow than in anger said: "By the sound and look of you, Jenny, you've poured a river of whisky down your own thrapple this night, my lass. And none of it good Scotch malt whisky either. But rather the cheap and nasty variety likely made in some hovel of a shebeen!"

Ever on the defensive and half out of her mind on cheap booze, as Kate had already surmised, Jenny – still swaying on her feet – fought back with the words: "Aye, but it's not the demon drink we're talking about, now is it. Mammy? It's men! First of all, you get your hooks into Terence when you knew damn well that it was me he was lusting after and not an old hag like you! And now what do you do? You just get yourself another fancy man! And here you are all cosying up with this stranger. Talk aboot my behaviour.

Uch, you disgust me, Mammy."

At these words, Danny rose to his feet and, stabbing an admonitory finger at Jenny, he shouted: "That's more than enough, Madam! Listen, Jenny Kinnon, don't you dare speak to your Mother like that."

Through her alcoholic mist, Jenny peered at the man standing before her.

"Oh? And just who the hell do you think you are? Listen, pal, I'll speak to my ragpicker of a mother any damned way I like."

Danny bunched his fingers into a fist and for a moment the situation looked ugly. Then after taking a deep breath he said: "I don't think I'm anyone different from what I am. But, listen here, my fine lady ... don't let this beard and the tropical tan fool you in any way. She's my mother too. And don't you ever forget it. I'm telling you this, and telling you once only, mess my mother about, and you'll have me to answer to. And believe me, I'm a force to be reckoned with. I've travelled the world and come out fighting with worse rogues than you'd ever meet in a lifetime of pub crawling through Glasgow's darkest drinking dens. So, like I say, leave my dear mother in peace, you disgusting, drunken apology for a dutiful daughter."

Chapter 8

In the days following Danny's visit, relations between Kate and Jenny were, if possible, even more strained than usual. And to make matters even worse, Jenny, obviously aware of what a fool she had made of herself before her brother, went sulking around the house.

All that was bad enough, but Kate was terrified that unwittingly she would let the cat out of the bag in an unguarded moment of conversation and disclose to the world the ultimate shame of a drunken daughter. Ever since the disastrous soiree and its aftermath Jenny had been drinking heavily. Kate shuddered to think where she was getting the money for her whisky but frequently Jenny arrived home late in the evening staggering drunk.

During a couple of tea breaks at Mac's Restaurant, Kate was sorely tempted to confide in Betty.

However, they had been close friends for so long that Betty knew some matter of importance was being withheld. When she could hold her tongue no longer, Betty leant across the table, laid a hand on Kate's arm and said: "Listen old pal of mine. Ah know somethin's botherin' ye ..."

Kate started to shake her head but Betty was having none of it.

"Deny it aw ye want. But ye'll not fob me off. So, come on, out with it."

Casting a glance over her shoulder to make sure neither Alec nor Auld Mac were nearby, Kate, with the air of a conspirator, beckoned her friend closer and after a second's hesitation she started to whisper in Betty's ear.

Betty gasped in amazement. "Kate! Ye dinnae mean it. What on earth possessed the lass? Comin home in a state like that. God alone knows where she'd been or even what scum she's been cavorting around wi. My God, if her drinkin's got to that stage, ye'll need tae get help o some kind. Mind ye, if she's in the family way again, there's naethin Ah would be willin' to help wi on that score."

Later that day Kate was glad she had been circumspect about Jenny's drinking problem. The main rush hour past, local shopkeepers from the Govan Road dropped in for their mid-day meal. Kate, in the past, had wondered why the restaurant wasn't bothered by drunks when the many public houses in and around Elder Street closed and emptied at two o'clock.

That afternoon, just on two, a drunk staggered in while Auld Mac was out of sight in the kitchen. The drunk slumped onto the nearest bench. If he had kept reasonably quiet nothing might have happened, but he lurched to his feet again and made his way noisily to a table closer to the kitchen. Auld Mac appeared at the door just as the drunk stumbled close. Auld Mac's bushy moustache bristled, his face turned red, a vein throbbed in his left temple. With an ear splitting roar he stepped forward.

"Out! Out! I'll have no drink sodden wretch in my restaurant."

The drunk swayed uncertainly. "Keep yer hair on, Mac. Ah'm no drunk. Just a wee bit happy. A cup o tea an a plate o' mince'll see me fine."

"Out, I said! And out you'll go –"

"Aye, that'll be right. Wha'll mak me go?"

"Me."

"Oh, aye? Ye and what army?"

"Alec, the door! Open the door wide." Auld Mac shouted.

Auld Mac spun the drunk round and, gripping him by the seat of his pants and the collar of his jacket, rushed him through the restaurant and out the door. A final thrust sent him sprawling onto his face on the pavement.

Hands on hips, Auld Mac glared down at his would-be customer. "Stay out. I don't want to see your face in here again."

Turning back into the restaurant, his moustache still bristling and his face almost purple, Auld Mac said: "I'll not have anyone in here showing drink taken."

He stamped back into the kitchen where Kate and Betty exchanged glances.

Betty whispered: "He's dead against drink."

She glanced out into the restaurant. "Oh Lord, he's the last thing we need right noo. Wi Auld Mac already aw riled up this could be a right terr."

"Why?" Kate said. "What's his problem?"

"He bitches aboot everythin. If he maks too big a fuss the day wi Auld Mac like he is Ah dinnae ken what'll happen."

Betty rushed out to take the newcomer's order. Back in the kitchen with a wink at Kate and a wary eye on Auld Mac she said: "He'll have the soup, if it's no too salty ..."

Auld Mac's moustache bristled and Betty rushed on: "... and the mince if it's no too watery the day."

Alec blew out his cheeks and on Auld Mac's face the colour, which had begun to fade, intensified.

"He'll have his tea wi his mince, because he's in a hurry."

About twenty minutes later Betty came into the kitchen carrying a cup of tea, with the spoon still in the cup, on its saucer.

"He says his tea's cauld."

Without a word, Auld Mac snatched the cup off the saucer and placed it, still with the spoon in it, on the hottest part of the cast iron cooking surface almost over the fire. He stood patiently until the tea in the cup started to boil, then holding the cup with an oven mitt he placed it carefully on a fresh saucer.

Following Betty back into the restaurant he watched her place the cup and saucer in front of the customer, who frowned at the spoon still sticking up in the cup then grasped it.

With an oath and: "My God, that's boiling!" the spoon sailed through the air, just missing Auld Mac.

"Is your tea hot enough now?"

As the customer stamped out, having thrown his money on the counter, he snarled: "I'll never eat here again."

"That'll be too soon," Auld Mac said, and glared at the other laughing customers.

Kate hid herself in the corner of the kitchen, unable to stifle her laughter, but when Auld Mac came in he was smiling.

"Let's all have some tea. I should have done that weeks ago."

And then it was back to work. So much so, that Kate and Betty had not a minute to spare either for idle chit-chat or the exchanging of confidences. As Kate made her way home on the tramcar, she reflected that although she had not as yet been able to impart the full extent of the problem with Jenny, at least she had told Betty enough to elicit sympathy, compassion, and a quickly whispered word of where and how Kate might go about getting professional help.

Added to the glow of satisfaction was the inner sense of happiness which Kate felt knowing that once home there would be some measure of peace. Jenny had already said she would be going out and tonight would leave Theresa and Hannah with Granny before leaving to meet her friends. So Kate knew at least in the empty house, she would be able to have a cup of tea in peace and quiet before her own visitor would arrive. Kate had not told Jenny of Terence's planned visit for supper.

As she let herself into the silent flat, Kate smiled to herself and also made a firm resolve to follow the line of help as suggested by Betty. After all, if anyone should know about the trials of drink within a family, it was surely Betty. Not only had her father been a roaring alcoholic, but it was rumoured that Betty's husband was not averse to spending the bulk of his Friday pay poke in his favourite drinking howff before staggering home to give his hardworking wife the ritual Friday night battering to ensure that she kept on working and also to reinforce the fact of who was the boss in their household.

Kate tried to switch off mentally as she looked forward to a blether and a spot of poetry reading with Terence.

Chapter 9

Kate stood in the morning chill awaiting the tramcar which would take her over to Govan and another day's honest toil. Once aboard, as always on the top deck of the tram, she settled as comfortably as she could. That done, she loosened her shawl and withdrew from her apron packet a small notebook and a stub of pencil. Kate licked the blunt lead, opened her notebook and at once started writing.

Ever since Dr Clancy, years before, had told Kate to find a hobby, she had been an avid reader. As the breadth of her interests increased and she read more widely, she had began to feel that she too could write. Even before Pearce's death she started to write in any of her few private minutes – *a secret vice,* she told herself, not even Terence knew, but often she wondered if she would ever dare show her writings to anyone, let alone publish them.

She scribbled frantically, writing until, with a start, she realised that the tram was nearing Govan Cross. Hastily looking around to see if her activities has been observed, Kate closed the notebook and shoved it back into her pocket. She smiled with quiet satisfaction when it dawned on her, that doubtless weighed down with their own life's problems, other people were less than interested in her or her precious notebook.

When she got off the tram at the foot of Elder Street, Kate thought: *At least this helps to keep my mind occupied. Stop me thinking so much about Jenny and my other problems.*

As she stepped out along the road, another thought struck her: *Just one thing! I'll just have to see that Betty doesn't get wind of what I'm up to. She'd never understand, not in a month of Sundays, and she would tease the life out of me. Mind you, I suppose she will wheedle it out of me one of these days. But for the moment, my guilty secret is safe.*

And with that comforting thought safely lodged in her brain, Kate stepped out with renewed vigour for the chores that awaited her at Auld Mac's Workmen's Restaurant.

The frantic rush of the workmen's dinner break was over for another day. Now it was Kate's duty to set out mugs of sweetened tea for Auld Mac, Alec, Betty, and herself. This was as much part of the daily ritual as the mounds of dirty dishes and stacks of pots which kept Kate busy in the restaurant kitchen. Her work station at the steel sink was directly below the iron-barred window overlooking the middens of the back-court, so her few minutes of freedom in the front shop with a mug of tea was always more than welcome. Once settled at one of the long bench tables, Betty leant forward and said: "A lovely cup of tea, Kate. And thank God we can take the weight aff oor feet for a wee while."

Kate smiled her agreement and her friend went on: "But sair feet and achin back apart, Kate, are ye glad you took on this wee job?"

At these words, Kate's eyes filled with tears. She gulped, then said: "Glad? Glad did you say, Betty? It's been my salvation! And it's all thanks to you. That was awful good of you to put in a kind word for me with Auld Mac."

Betty took a sip of her tea. "Well, the auld so-n-so, he's a hard taskmaster, Ah'll tell ye that. But then, ye yersel ye've never been afraid of hard work in any shape or form. So, Ah had a good idea ye'd fit in well here. Just one thing worries me a wee bit …"

As her words trailed off, Kate, with a frown of anxiety already on her face, said: "Oh, Betty! Don't tell me Auld Mac isn't pleased with me. I'm doing my level best. Even though it near breaks my back lifting those iron cauldrons he calls soup-pots. But my God! If I was to lose this job ..."

Betty silenced the flow of words with a hand on Kate's arm as she said: "Kate! Kate! Will ye stop haverin on. What Ah was goin tae say ... Ah'm jist a wheen worried that the travellin frae Candleriggs tae Govan every day ... is it no mibbe too tirin for ye? For let's face it, ye're looking kinda washed-oot this mornin. Ah widnae like it aw tae be too much for ye."

"No, Betty, this is a grand job and I wouldn't give it up for anything. It's just that I still help out at the paper shop on our street and I'm out real early to open the shop for him for the first customers. I'll be fine."

"It's high time that Jenny of yours did something to bring in some money and take some of the load."

"Jenny does have a wee job. She cleans for a house in Montieth Row. It's not much but it does bring in something."

Kate didn't add that it was only one day a week – Saturdays – and Jenny was not overly keen on cleaning work.

Chapter 10

It was the start of another working day and, as Kate turned the corner into Elder Street, she stopped dead in her tracks. Hardly able to believe her eyes, she stared in amazement at the knot of people gathered round the nearside window of Mac's Workman's Restaurant. As she hurried across to the shop, she wondered: *What on earth is going on? And at this hour of the morning. I hope nothing's wrong.*

Arriving at the shop, she was hard pressed to push her way through the crowd of spectators. But even so, not one person moved so much as an inch to enable her to catch sight of whatever it was in the window that was exciting their attention. On all sides, she could hear grown men, hefty workmen at that, oohing and aahing in wonder and calling out.

"Heh, Jimmy! Did ye e'er see the likes of that?"

"Aye! Trust Auld Mac to come up with somethin different."

"Wattie! Ah don't knew aboot ye, but Ah for yin could jist staun here aw day, fair gawpin in wonder at them."

Wattie's friend laughed. "Aye, jist ye dae that, Hashie! And when the work's hooter gaes, don't ye bother yer bunnet, in fact don't ye worry yer bluidy heid. Leave it aw tae me, pal. Ah'll jist explain tae the gaffer. Ah'll tell him that Hashie Dodds'll no be intae his work the day … he's got a heavy date, winchin three daft wee pigs."

His other workmates roared with laughter and there was much back-slapping, tip-tilting of tweed bunnets and general hilarity in the group as they continued to gaze in wonder at Auld Mac's shop window.

Knowing that the sound of the work's hooter would put paid soon enough to their harmless enjoyment of whatever peep show it was, Kate left them to it and made her way inside the shop.

Alec, as usual, was hard at work preparing the day's cauldron of soup. Auld Mac, flushed with triumph, was like a dog with two tails as Betty sang his praises.

"Honestly, Mac, Ah jist don't know how ye think it aw up. Bloody genius, so ye are."

Alec looked up from his contemplation of the soup. "Aye, Auld yin, right enough. Ah've got to hand it to ye. There's no another shop window like it in the whole o' Govan, or Glesga either, for aw Ah ken."

Unable to contain her curiosity a moment longer, Kate burst in with: "Listen, you lot ... will somebody please tell me what all the fuss is about? For thanks to the crowds out there, I couldn't get within a mile of the window. Mibbe you've even nicked the Honours of Scotland and got those treasures sitting nice as ninepence in there."

Three pairs of eyes turned to stare at her and if none them knew exactly what the Honours of Scotland were, they were not about to signpost their ignorance of Scottish history. However, Auld Mac, aware he had a captive audience, laid a hand on Kate's shoulder and led her gently out of the kitchen. Then, with all the aplomb of a master magician, he pointed dramatically to the window display. Kate gasped. Centre-stage were three earthenware pigs, each one standing tall and proud on two little trotters while the other two trotters had been fashioned to hold rods which in turn held long glass trays of Auld Mac's apple tarts, Scotch ashet pies, and Johnston's mutton pies. One pig, obviously the gaffer, wore a garish checked waistcoat and a boss's bowler hat; while the other two workers sported long white aprons, such as both Alec and Auld Mac himself wore for their daily darg of cooking and baking in the kitchen and for doling out jugs of hot soup and plates of mince and tatties at the carrying-out counter.

Later that same morning over a specially extended celebratory tea-break, when the talk was still about his wonderful advertising feature, Auld Mac leant forward and said: "Aye! It's true what ye were saying earlier, Betty. Most shop windows in Govan look like bluebottle graveyards. But I must be honest ... when trade was beginning to get a wee bit slack, I knew I had to do something to drum up a bit o' business. So, I got the idea of dressing the window in some way. And mind ye, it's all been done before ... not with the pigs I admit but years ago in the East End a chap called Lipton – he became a millionaire – he used to put weird and wonderful items in his window. He always had an eye-catching display. Drew men, women, and bairns from all round and at the same time, he fairly boosted his sales."

Kate, always keen to further her knowledge of whatever subject was under discussion, admitted that, yes, she had heard of Tommy Lipton but was unaware as to what particular advertising gems he had devised.

Auld Mac smiled with the air of one about to impart his superior learning. "Kate, lass, if I was to tell ye Lipton's whole story ye'd have a much longer tea break than I've already granted ye this day. But one thing I will tell ye ... he deserved to become a millionaire, that man. At one point, he'd put a bloody great cheese in his window with a notice telling folk that it contained of aw things golden sovereigns! So, poverty-stricken Glesga folk were fighting to buy a hunk o' cheese, then straight out in the street tearing at it with their bare hands and chewing carefully in the hope of making a fortune.

Alec laughed. "Weel, Mac, somehow I don't think ye'll be throwing away sovereigns, nor hauf-croons either, tae the folk o Govan. But one thing for sure ... it looks like yer display will soon be drawing the crowds like a magnet. So, ye never ken, mibbe ye're another Tommy Lipton in the making."

There was general hilarity at this point. Then Betty, doubtless feeling that more than enough praise had already been heaped on Auld Mac's head risking him getting puffed up with ideas of untold grandeur, leant forward. "Aw very interesting. But wonderful as it aw is … Ah'm … well … to be perfectly honest, Ah'm thinking that there's mibbe one wee thing missing."

Total silence greeted this criticism, together with a beetle-browed glower from the hero of the hour. One and all, they waited for Betty to go on. With a wicked grin at Kate, she nodded sagely. "What it needs … jist tae put the finishing touch, ye understand … is a wee poem of some kind. Aye! That's the very dab, a wee verse that'll explain to folk jist whit the pigs are supposed tae be daein – apart from jist staunin' there looking all swanky and fine and dandy."

Mac slapped a hand to his brow, as if he had suddenly seen the wisdom of Betty's pronouncement. Threatening frown gone in an instant, he now grinned widely.

"Betty! Ye're no jist a pretty face, are ye, hen? Ye've got a guid heid on ye. Aye. That's it. So, not a minute tae be wasted. My lassie, this very night just ye get busy and write us a special wee poem."

Betty giggled in almost girlish-like glee. "Aw here! Haud oan a meenit, Mac. Ah might be mony a thing, but one thing Ah'm no … and that's a bloody poet. It wisnae me Ah was thinkin aboot. But mind you, there is somebody no a thousand miles frae here … writes rerr poetry."

Alec and Auld Mac looked puzzled. Kate felt her cheeks burn as she wondered how on earth Betty had discovered her secret, her guilty secret she had divulged to no-one, not even to Granny Gorbals. All those stories and poems she had scribbled on her way to and from Govan on the tramcar. But somehow Betty had known all along.

That was it! The day she found the notepad in the wrong pocket on her way home. She'd wondered about that then assumed it must have happened in her rush to get off the tram.

And now, much to Kate's acute embarrassment, here was her so-called best friend urging her to write a poem ... and of all things, a poem about three stupid wee ceramic pigs.

The final indignity, her ultimate literary outpouring was destined to be displayed in a shop window in the mean streets of Govan. Not her envisaged literary fame.

When it began to look as if all their entreaties would fail, Auld Mac took a firmer hand in the proceedings and negotiations. "Tell me this, Kate. Have ye ever had any of yer writing published?"

Kate shook her head dolefully. "Published? Chance would be a fine thing. Who in their right mind would want to publish any of my literary outpourings?"

Auld Mac leant across the table and speaking directly to her said: "Chance did ye say? And isn't that exactly what I'm offering ye now? Tell ye what ..."

Here he drew Kate closer and whispered for her ears only.

Kate blinked in astonishment. "Oh, Mr Mac, you don't mean it? That would be a dream come true."

Auld Mac nodded. "Right, lass, that's settled. The minute ye get home tonight just ye sit yerself doon and write me that poem. And remember ..." Here he tapped the side of his nose. The gesture alone – quite apart from his bearing – sealed the bargain they had made.

At the same time it had the added bonus of excluding Betty and Alec. With a cursory glance at them, Auld Mac said: "That pair will find out all in good time."

And find out they did, as did the entire population of Govan when a well printed leaflet with, of all things, a poem by Kate Kinnon came fluttering through each and every letterbox in every single tenement in the district. Having read this seven days wonder, who could possibly resist the lure of Auld Mac's three pigs and their sales pitch poem?

It was the talk of the steamie as local parlance had it. Quite apart from every household having their own copy of the poem, it was displayed in all its glory alongside the pigs in the shop window.

Here in Mac's window
What do you see?
Three little pigs
Happy as can be
Our work we willingly do
Holding Mac's pies
All ready for you
So why don't you
Just give them a try
For cheap at the price
They're a very good buy
Then soon enough
Your ain guid man and bonnie bairns too
Our tuppenny pies
Will all happily chew
So hurry on now
Put on your shawl
We'll serve you gladly
Whenever you call

The end result of this massive advertising campaign was that for the first time ever, Kate saw some of her writing in print – not quite the literary masterpiece she would have liked but hadn't she read someplace a famous writer when asked what he wrote replied: "Anything anyone will pay me to write!"

Kate became something of a local celebrity and perhaps more importantly, Auld Mac sold even more of his wares and for the moment at least the slackness of trade with its threat of job loss for Betty and Kate was reversed.

One way and another, all things considered, Kate thought, *what more did life have to offer?*

Chapter 11

An early spring day, with the trees on the Glasgow Green beginning to show buds, greeted Kate as she set out for Monteith Row to yet again cover for Jenny's inability to rouse herself for her work.

As Kate left the close-mouth, she settled her shawl round her shoulders and mentally prepared herself for what lay ahead. There was a tight-lipped determination as she thought: *Well! Working for old Mrs Scott was never like this. But, the high-falutin Miss Anderson. Hmph: No wonder the old besom's got money. Every farthing's a prisoner.*

Arrived at the elegant townhouse in Monteith Row, Kate had little time to admire the spring colours across the road in the tree-lined Glasgow Green. Once admitted by the resident housekeeper to the ornate, overstuffed, over-furnished house, it was immediately a case of sleeves rolled up, heavy duty serge apron donned, and elbow grease into action. As she worked away at the myriad tasks set her by housekeeper, Mrs Dobson, Kate still had time to reflect on the past.

The very first day that Kate set foot on Scottish soil, she and Pearce had visited his aunt, the high-born Lady Christabel. And the hoity-toity madam had lived where? Where else but just further along this very same terrace.

About to go further down this tortuous path of memory, Kate's thoughts were interrupted by a voice at her elbow: "Kate, when you've finished the silver, come away into the kitchen for a wee cup of tea. Her Highness Madam Anderson is away to the Island of Bute to visit some of her equally grand but long-suffering relatives."

Needing no second bidding, Kate polished up the rest of the silver in double-quick time. The homely aroma of baking greeted her as she entered the kitchen, a well-stocked room in which a cheery fire was 'roarin up the lum' as Glasgow folk were wont to say.

Seating herself at the deal table, Kate laughed. "Judging by the healthy state of the fire, I think I'd have guessed that your mistress is away."

Mrs Dobson chuckled in ready agreement. "Aye: The old skinflint. Her idea of a good-going fire is one o yon coal briquette things banked with cinders and a ton of mouldy old tea leaves."

As the two women settled to their tea, a tasting of Mrs Dobson's celebrated Victoria cream sponge, and a good old blether, so happy were they in that moment that neither woman, to use the good old Glasgow phrase, would have 'called the King ma cousin'.

Having had their say about the many money-saving eccentricities of their employer, and having put the wider world furth of Glasgow to rights, they next turned to more immediate family matters.

"So, my dear, since you're here again in Jenny's place, I suppose: it's the usual problem with the poor wee soul? These terrible sick headaches she keeps getting."

Kate gulped a couple of times before trusting herself to speak. At last, she said: "You've certainly got that one right, Mrs Dobson. And let me say again how grateful I am for your understanding. It's so good of you."

Mrs Dobson waved aside Kate's words, already well aware of how vital to the Kinnon family budget was the money from Jenny's Saturday cleaning job here in Monteith Row.

"Now just you listen, Kate, my dear. We none of us know how

we would cope if faced with such a battery of problems as you have."

Even the sympathetic tone without the kind words would have been enough to bring tears to Kate's eyes. So, before she would be reduced to a sobbing wreck, she put out a hand to stem the flow of well-meaning words from her friend. Even then, it was a moment or two before she could force herself to voice her innermost thoughts. But of one thing she was certain ... she would have to tell this kind woman the truth, the absolute truth ... nothing else would do. She remembered her agonies of conscience over the lies to Etta Henderson about the matinee jackets and the embarrassing scene resulting from the incident with the puff candy and Tommy Boyde's teeth. Etta had remained her friend although she would have nothing more to do with Jenny.

At last Kate smiled through her tears and said: "I suppose we all have our problems in life. And we just struggle along with them in the best way we can."

Mrs Dobson gave a sympathetic smile and a nod of encouragement for her friend to go on.

"Yes, problems by the barrow load. But if I'm being strictly honest ... my main problem ... my biggest concern is with Jenny at the moment. You see, these terrible ..."

"Oh, my dear, Kate. You certainly don't need to tell me anything about sick bilious headaches, I've been a martyr to them all my life. And totally exhausting and nerve-wracking they are."

Kate was tempted to leave matters there, but she knew in her heart of hearts that, in the name of friendship, she had to tell the truth.

But before Kate could finally put into words what must be told, Mrs Dobson leant forward and, laying a kindly hand on Kate's arm, said: "But, she's young, so she may yet grow out of those headaches. But to turn to a cheerier matter, has that Jenny lass of yours got herself a man yet?"

Kate paused before speaking in case she blurted out that Jenny in her short life had been just too good at finding men and she had a bastard bairn to show for her efforts. So, keeping her own counsel, Kate in a mock gesture raised her eyes to heaven and said: "Uch, don't mention Jenny and men to me, Mrs Dobson. The man to please her hasn't yet been born on this earth."

Mrs Dobson tutted her sympathy, thus encouraging Kate further to unburden herself.

"You know, I even told her the other day. It's high time she was getting to be less choosy. For there's many a decent, good wage-earning man wearing a flat bunnet. They don't all have to be gaffers swanking about in a bowler hat."

Mrs Dobson nodded in agreement. "You're right there, Kate. It's perfectly true, that old Scots saying about never letting the bunnets go by while you're looking for a bowler or a top hat."

A fresh pot of tea, an extra helping of cream sponge and another shovelful of coal on the fire and the two women were well set up for a real heart-to-heart. When they had exhausted the topic of Jenny and her aversion to much housework and her disdain of the common working man, by mutual – if silent – agreement, they changed the subject. Soon Mrs Dobson was regaling Kate with a long and involved tale about her neer-do-weel brother-in-law and his latest get-rich scheme, together with his heavy-handed hints that all would be well, "If only he had the money to buy himself a barra."

"Well, says I to him, so you think if I has that kind of sillar, I'd be handing it ower to the likes of you? Far less be a widow woman working my fingers to the bone for an old skinflint like meanie Marigold Anderson. I'd be oot there wheeling a barra myself."

Kate smiled and not least at the mental picture of the physically well-endowed Mrs Dobson, like some kind of latter-day Molly Malone, wheeling her wheelbarrow through the streets broad and narrow of the Second City of the Empire.

Catching the twinkle in Kate's eyes and picturing herself as some sort of fishwife complete with bugle, bunnet, and barrow, she too collapsed in helpless laughter.

With the pair of them giggling like a pair of mischievous schoolgirls, Kate realized that she had lost the moment to tell the housekeeper the truth about Jenny's all too frequent bouts of 'bilious headaches'. Anyway, perhaps it was just as well not to disclose the real problem yet awhile. With any luck, Jenny by some miracle might stay sober on the coming Friday night and thus be able to present herself for work on the Saturday morning.

Later, as Kate said goodbye, Mrs Dobson shoved a cloth-wrapped bundle into her hand

"Here ye are, Kate … Just a few tasty sweetbites for your wee family. And the last of the cream sponge for Granny Gorbals. It'll be nice and soft for her auld gums, she'll no need to bite, just sook awa at it."

With their shared laughter ringing in her ears, Kate made her way back along Monteith Row. With every step she took, her resolve hardened to follow Mrs Dobson's advice in trying to get Jenny to apply for another wee part-time job Mrs Dobson had heard about in Partick, where her cousin was a hall caretaker and was on the lookout for a good worker to come in and do some cleaning for a couple of days every week. Mrs Dobson, bless her, had formed the opinion that if Jenny had more with which to occupy herself and at the same time, bring in more money to the family's housekeeping purse, then she would have less time to dwell on her sick headaches.

While Kate was determined to proffer that bit of advice, she would not however be in any way inclined to mention Mrs Dobson's tried and tested method of alleviating the misery of a bilious headache. Kate knew in her heart of hearts that it would take a lot more than a damp rag soaked in vinegar to cure Jenny's ailments. She didn't know what, if anything, was the right cure for a hangover, but she did know it would have to be something a deal stronger than a vinegar cloth. Kate knew she was still unhappy about having lied to her friend about the nature of Jenny's illness, but perhaps she need never again sin her soul in this way.

Meantime, in a more cheerful mood, she went up to her flat secure in the knowledge that Granny and the bairns would most certainly enjoy to the full the contents of the tasty-bite bag which Mrs Dobson had so kindly sent for them. Yes, all things considered, perhaps everything had worked out for the best after all. Buoyed up with the optimism of the moment and the kindness shown her by Mrs Dobson, that very night Kate read Jenny such a lecture that it was bound to have some result. It did. Jenny crashed out of the house in a tantrum, finishing her onslaught of words with: "Look, Mother. It's my life and if I want to enjoy a wee refreshment on a Friday night, it's none of your bloody business. And if you can't stop me, then sure as hell no holier-then-thou, Mrs fucking Dobson, is going to stand in my way either. So, come next Saturday, if anybody's going to Monteith Row, it looks like it'll have to be you again. Got it?"

"Listen, Mrs Dobson, Angusina, if I may, there's something I must tell you. Well, not to put too fine point on it … it's hangovers Jenny suffers from. If only it had been honest-to-God headaches … that I could have coped with …"

With the truth finally out in the open, Kate gave a sigh of relief. But if she was relieved, the stark truth which she had just blurted out was having a totally different effect on Mrs Dobson. After an intake of breath, the housekeeper leant forward and stared at Kate.

When Mrs Dobson's words finally came, gone was the kindly inflection, and so also were all traces of compassion from her face.

"Oh, drink: The Demon Drink. Is that what you are telling me? That curse has made a mockery, a ruin of many a person's life. And let's face it, even being associated with it, look what it's done to you, Mistress Kinnon. You've even had to lie to me. Hmph. And here was me a martyr to bilious headaches all my life, being all sympathetic to Jenny, thinking she was a fellow sufferer. And even taking on the responsibility of allowing you to take her place."

In the silence that followed, Kate knew instinctively what Mrs Dobson's next words would be.

No matter how Kate argued, cajoled, and even finally begged, the housekeeper would not be moved from her resolve. There would be no further employment in Miss Anderson's strictly teetotal home – either for Jenny or her mother – and that was final.

When Kate left Monteith Row that morning, the glory of the spring sunshine was lost on her. She reflected sadly that thanks to Jenny, the Kinnon family had lost yet another source of income and she had lost face in telling deliberate lies in order to cover for Jenny. Even worse, she knew this time she had lost a friend.

Chapter 12

Arriving at her flat after her day at Auld Mac's, Kate found it empty and after a quick knock on Granny Gorbals' door she walked in expecting to find Hannah and Theresa there as usual. At the sight that greeted her she stopped short in the doorway.

"Terence, Danny, what are you two doing here?"

"We arrived at the close at the same time," Danny said, "and Granny Gorbals heard us knocking on your door."

"We've introduced ourselves, Kate," Terence said. "Although I'd have known this young man anywhere without introduction. He's the spitting image of Pearce as he was when he worked in the market."

"When did you see Pearce?" Kate asked puzzled. Terence had never mentioned meeting Pearce.

"Often when he worked in the market. Before I ever met you. I was in the market getting produce for my other barrows. After we met, and you mentioned his name, I asked around at the market. Lots of people remembered him."

"Wait a minute," Kate said. "You said 'your barrows'. The Market doesn't deal in books."

Terence laughed. "No, but I don't just have the book barrow. It happens to be the one I like to work at."

Danny had been looking back and forth from Terence to his mother during this exchange with a frown on his face. He seemed about to say something, but Terence continued: "I called up to tell you I'll be away for a couple of days, but I'll drop in as soon as I get back. I'll go now; I'm sure you and Danny have a lot to say to each other."

Terence turned. "Thanks, Granny, for the tea." He put his hand out to Danny. "I suppose I'll be seeing quite a bit of you while you're in port, but I'll say goodbye for now."

Danny didn't shake Terence's hand. Terence shrugged and walked out.

"You and Danny go on through," Granny Gorbals said. "I'm sure you've a lot to talk about and I'll keep Hannah and wee Theresa here for a bit."

In her flat, Kate turned to Danny.

"Now what was wrong with your face in Granny's? You were downright rude to Terence; not taking his hand when he offered it."

"Now listen, Mother, far be it from me to criticise ... but I don't think you should be encouraging that Terence character to come around the house quite so much as I've heard he does."

"And exactly why should that be?"

"Well, let's face it, Mother ... the fellow is nothing other than a common barrow boy. And most certainly not fit company for a widow ... a decent widow woman of your high social standing."

"High social standing? High social standing be damned. Listen to me, Danny Kinnon. I've had to go out cleaning other people's stairs and closes – yes, even their stair-head lavatories – I've been a ragpicker; I've cleaned houses like the servant I am; now I'm a skivvy and dishwasher in a working man's restaurant. All to keep body and soul together. Does that sound like a widow of high social standing? Look round you. Is this the posh residence of a widow of high social standing? Hah! A decent widow of high social standing be damned."

"Have it your own way, Mother. But just don't you ever forget this ... for all his faults, my late-lamented father was a gentleman.

So with his having dragged you up from the gutter and having married you, then, by association, you became socially superior to the common herd. So please do not despoil my father's memory with meeting up with a slum layabout and barrow boy like Terence O'Neil."

"Your father's memory! My God, you've changed your tune. When you first came home after his death you admitted you couldn't stand him."

"That's a different matter. What I felt about him personally doesn't alter the fact that he was a gentleman born and as such entitled to the respect due a gentlemen – the respect due to him by his widow."

"This from you that ran away to sea to get away from him – a common before-the-mast seaman."

Danny shrugged. "Well, maybe I did get a bit carried away about our social standing, but I still think a barrow boy is beneath you –"

"Yes, Terence is a barrow boy in the sense that he runs a book barrow. But we heard today that he owns more than one barrow, didn't we? He's a businessman. But he is a cultured, caring, well-read Irish gentleman. As for being uneducated ... why, he could quote reams of the most beautiful poetry and, if you remember, that was something your late-lamented, cultured saint of a father considered the mark of a gentleman."

"Mammy, I don't want to quarrel with you. I'm sorry if what I said offended you. But it is what I truly think and you always taught me to speak my mind."

"Think what you like, Danny. That's your right, but I'll not be dictated to by you. I had a bellyful of that when your father was alive. I'll do as I please and as I see fit. I'll not give up Terence to please you, so you can either accept that and him or stay away."

"I'll be going then, Mammy. I'd best be back on board – I'm a bit past being just a common before-the-mast seaman – I'm in charge of men now."

With that Danny left and Kate collapsed into the armchair, emotionally drained.

Exactly how, when, and why had her beloved son, her own darling Danny, grown to become such an insufferable, opinionated snob? For there was just no other way to describe the man he had shown himself to be today.

Suddenly the awful thought came: *Perhaps it had all stemmed from that childish escapade at the Exhibition in 1888 when Hannah, stuffed with sweets by Danny, had been sick in the posh restaurant. Pearce had thrashed Danny mercilessly while raging: "We are not Irish scum. Poverty stricken or not, we are still people of quality. Don't you ever forget that, Daniel Kinnon."*

Kate gave a long, heartfelt sigh as she thought: *My poor Danny Boy. Perhaps you never did forget that lesson ... and that has made you what you are today. Who knows?*

Rousing herself, Kate threw some cold water on her face and trudged next door to Granny Gorbals' flat.

"Well? What was the news that Danny had for ye?" Granny Gorbals asked as soon as Kate walked in.

"News? He didn't have any news that I know of. He just miscalled Terence and tried to warn me off him. Did he say to you that he had some news?"

Granny Gorbals frowned and shook her head. "He said he had to speak to you –"

"Oh, he spoke to me all right. Nonsense about Terence being beneath me. That I, 'a widow of high social standing', should be careful who I associate with –"

Kate was interrupted by Granny Gorbals' cackling laugh.

"Oh, we're that aw right, widows o' high standin, we couldnae be any higher could we? Unless we stood on the roof."

For a moment Kate continued to look serious, then joined in Granny Gorbals' laughter.

"Right, Granny, it's best to laugh. Did he say what he wanted to talk to me about?"

"No, he didnae seem to want to tell in front o Terence, but he seemed a bit on edge aboot it."

"Well, whatever it was, it's too late now. He's gone back to his ship."

"Dinnae worry yersel aboot it. And dinnae worry aboot him and Terrence. Ah'm sure when they get to ken each other they'll get on just fine."

"Whether they do or not, it'll be Danny's problem. I'll not let him take over where Pearce left off. He can like it or lump it."

"That's the stuff, Kate."

Several days later, Kate answered the door to find Danny on the landing.

"Can I come in, Mammy?"

Kate nodded and led the way through to the kitchen.

"I need to talk with you before I have to sail again. I know we didn't part on the best of terms last time …"

"No, we didn't. You sounded just like your father at his worst."

Danny coughed. "Yes, I'm sorry if I upset you, but I had to say what was on my mind. I told you I'd signed up with a company that sails out of Glasgow and that I've decided to get a wee single-end someplace near the docks –"

"I told you before, there's no need to do that. I said you'd be welcome here for your stay in port."

"Well, the fact is … I've already taken one …" He stopped and flushed.

"Why don't we sit down and have a cup of tea. Terence will be here soon –"

"Mammy, haven't you given any thought to we talked about last time. Terence is beneath you –"

Kate exploded. "Now just you listen here, Daniel Kinnon. We

did not talk about it last time. You lectured. I'll not be dictated again by any man about 'my position in society'. Terence is my friend and if you don't like that then you can stay away."

"Mammy, you might hear some gossip in Govan –"

"I'll hear no more from you, Daniel Kinnon. I think you should leave now."

Red-faced, Danny shrugged and left.

Chapter 13

Kate was beginning to feel that, at last, perhaps life was settling down into some more peaceful pattern for her and her family. After the highs and lows of unlooked-for domestic drama over the past years, the humdrum passing of days which contained nothing other than work, marketing, and an occasional blether to her neighbours was nothing short of paradise on earth for her. And wonder of wonders, even her rebel daughter Jenny now seemed to be on a more tranquil path of life. Thus Kate mused as she gazed into the flickering firelight, while at the same time admitting that, despite their parting squabble, she did miss her beloved Danny. But, yes, one way and another, life was good.

Almost as if the gods who control such things had heard her thoughts and had decided that Kate Kinnon had no right to be in a peaceful haven, suddenly – within days – all hell had broken loose yet again.

The run of bad luck started at, of all places, Mac's Restaurant. While Kate could not put her finger on it, somehow she felt that her employers, and even her friend Betty, suddenly seemed to have a down on her. Kate knew that she was working as hard as ever; still working as cheerfully over the black iron sink with its everlasting mound of dirty dishes; and still as chirpy in her dealings with the workmen when she was serving at tables. But no matter how she tried to convince herself to the contrary, there was something ... an unresolved resentment, a feeling of antipathy hanging in the air but not as yet expressed in words. Kate felt the atmosphere around her, almost like a heavy tweed cloak enshrouding her being.

Had there been angry words, or even a meaningful glance passed between her work companions, this she could have challenged, brought out into the open, and then dealt with in her usual forthright manner. But this fog, this dark cloud of condemnation for she knew not what, this not only defeated her but wrapped her daily in feelings of doubt, desolation and dread. What in God's name had she done to upset these good people? Why had the wonderful sense of kitchen camaraderie and cheerful backchat so suddenly gone? And finally, what if anything could she do to restore matters to the former easy friendship?

After two days and long sleepless nights of such introspection Kate was beginning to feel at the end of her tether. Not only was she snapping and snarling at everyone who crossed her path, she felt also that her work was starting to suffer. And that, she knew, could not be allowed to go on, for she needed every hard-earned halfpenny of her wages from Mac's Restaurant.

On the tramcar home one Friday eight, Kate chewed at her lower lip as she worried again and again over yet another day of uneasy silences, strained atmosphere and averted glances. Then like a thunderbolt, it struck here

That's it! They're just like Danny. They're all hiding something from me. Same as he was. I felt he wanted to tell me something that last time. I just knew he wanted to confide in me – but just didn't dare!

As she wrestled with these thoughts, Kate's attention was momentarily diverted when two Friday night revellers, whose raucous singing had been entertaining their fellow passengers, suddenly started to get ugly. With much use of the overworked F-word, the two drunken men staggered to their feet and then roundly cursed everyone in sight for not having joined in with the chorus of their maudlin version of The Bonnie Wells o' Wearie. One of the unwilling audience said: "Awa hame tae yer wives, ye drunken eejits." And another added: "Aye, that's if youse have even a penny piece left in your paypackets." The remainder of the passengers wholeheartedly agreed that the poor wives waiting at home wouldn't have over much to sing about when their drunken, penniless, 'better halves' would finally stagger through the door.

Kate, while she continued to watch the antics of the two roaring drunks, kept aloof from the ongoing badinage. She had enough on her mind in grappling with the horrendous thought which had come unbidden into her mind.

Oh my God! Suddenly it's clear. I know! I just know exactly what Danny and all the others have been trying to hide from me. It's Jenny! Oh dear sweet Jesus ... it's Jenny, she's back on the booze again.

Once safely home through the gaslit city streets, vennels, and wynds all heaving with drunken humanity, Kate was in a fever of impatience to confront her daughter. But when, as yet, there was no sign of Jenny, Kate went through the motions of making a scratch meal for the family. By the time the kettle was boiling on the hob, Kate's temper was at the same fever pitch of eruption.

When it seemed to Kate she could restrain herself not a minute longer, Jenny walked in the door. Hardly had her daughter hung up her tammy on its hook, than Kate launched into the attack.

"Right, madam. So, what are you up to now? Just tell me that."

Jenny's eyes widened in astonishment at the unprovoked onslaught. But before she could utter a single word in her defence, Kate went on: "Back on the cheap booze again, are .you? And whoring around, if I'm not mistaken. Seems like your ill-gotten fame as a whisky sodden fallen woman has even travelled to Govan. Aye: Over there, decent folk can hardly bear to look at me – all thanks to you ... my darling daughter."

Jenny stood in stunned silence. She struggled to speak, but when no words came, she stared in horror at her mother. When it was clear from Kate's demeanour that she was about to renew the attack, at last Jenny managed to croak out: "Mammy! Fine well you know I've been trying hard recently. So, what on earth's got into you? Sounds to me like you are the one who's been on the bottle!"

Kate gasped.

"Don't you dare cast aspersions like that on my character, Jenny Kinnon. As well you know, the only whisky that ever passes my lips is a wee teaspoonful from the medicinal bottle. Anyway, it's you we're talking about, not me. Now, let's have no more of this nonsense! What do you have to say for yourself?"

Game to the last, Jenny stood her ground.

"Listen, Mammy. I haven't a bloody clue what the hell you're on about. And I'll say it again as God is my witness, all these past months, I've been trying and –"

Kate smiled grimly. "Trying, did you say? Oh yes, you've got that one right, you've been trying my patience and my sanity, ever since the day you were born. Anyway, let's have less of the foul language, my girl, and a bit more of the home truths. So … what filthy sink of iniquity have you waded into this time? Men and booze certainly. And what more besides?"

Jenny's face was white as chalk. Then, with trembling fingers, she turned away from her mother and lifted down her tammy. This she rammed on her head then, in a low voice in which every syllable was crystal clear, she said: "Right, Mammy, if that's what you think of me … I'm out of here. That's all the thanks I get for going along in secret to those meetings. And for signing the Pledge to try keep off the drink. To say nothing of living like a bloody nun."

After a tense silence Jenny said: "But before I take my wee Theresa and get the hell out of your face and out of your life, there's one thing I will say –"

"Oh indeed; and what might that be? For I doubt there's any single fact could ever change my opinion of you for the better, Jenny."

Jenny gave a sad little smile.

"Yes, Mammy. I do know exactly what you think of me. But what I wanted to say was this ... nobody in Govan knows anything about me but, on the other hand, what about your favourite? Aye, what about your beloved Danny Boy? Don't forget, his ship is often in the Govan docks. He's the one shaming you. Living in a single end in Govan with a darkie. Try that for size when you're thinking about respectability and gossip in Govan."

Jenny lifted Theresa in her arms. Then wrapping a worn tweed shawl around herself and her bairn, she left the house in Candleriggs.

The slamming of the outer door echoed in Kate's heart and mind for the rest of that interminable night. As she tossed and turned on her sleepless pillow, she worried and tormented herself.

Why could I not have held my tongue until I'd spoken to Betty? And got my facts right before I tackled Jenny.

Kate worried in those dark reaches of the night that she indeed might have misjudged Jenny. It was certainly true Jenny had been something of a reformed character of late. And now, with a barrage of hasty, ill-chosen words, Kate had destroyed at a single blow the better if slightly fragile relationship she had recently and miraculously been managing to build with her formerly errant daughter. Even so, she still could not accept Jenny's theory that dear Danny was in some way to blame for how matters currently stood over in Govan. Kate bit at her lip.

Three o'clock in the morning is the loneliest and the saddest time in the world for any insomniac ... and so it was for Kate Kinnon. Finally, in the cold light of dawn, when she could stand her mental torment not a moment longer, she eased herself from the bed which resembled a battlefield. She padded into the kitchen to make herself a pot of tea. She was tempted to add a spot of the water of life from the medicine bottle, but on reflection and in view what the fierce argument had been about, she thought better of it.

As she lifted the enamel mug to her lips, she suddenly thought: *That's just me and poor Hannah left: Jenny's gone and so has our dear wee Theresa. Is this what my life has all been about? Me left alone with a handicapped bairn. And not even a dictatorial husband to organise the household. Is all this misery my punishment for having taken Pearce from the bosom of his family? Dear God if ever a romantic elopement ended in total disaster, then mine surely did.*

Next morning Kate decided to bring matters into the open, so at the tea break she cleared her throat loudly, looked straight at Betty and said: "For the last couple of days I thought I'd done something to upset everybody –"

"Oh, no –" Betty started, but Kate waved her down.

"Let me finish. I thought it was something to do with Jenny, but when I tackled her last night she told me the problem was with Danny – he's living in Govan with a coloured girl."

There was a collective release of breath.

Alec smiled. "Sorry about the atmosphere the last few days, but we didn't know what to say. It's all round Govan. There's never been anyone like that in Govan before. We've seen plenty of those lascar sailors off the boats, of course, but never a girl like her – and living with one of us!"

"Aye, a real seven day's wonder," Betty said.

"Is no one going to do any work today?" Auld Mac said, and tea break was over.

That same evening Terence arrived. He took one look at Kate and said: "What's got you into such a stushie tonight? I thought things were going fairly well with you and Jenny."

Kate told him of the quarrel the night before and of Jenny's departure.

"... and it turns out it's all because of Danny's stupidity in bringing a heathen black girl to live with him in Govan."

Terence frowned. "We've never talked about it, I know, but I didn't think you were that bigoted. Your friend Betty is a Catholic, like me, and Pearce, as a High Anglican, wasn't a kick in the pants off being Catholic."

Kate glared at Terence. "What has that to do with Danny's girl?"

"Just that I don't think Father Ryan would be pleased at being called a heathen."

"Don't talk nonsense. It was *the girl* I said was heathen."

Terence shrugged. "There have been Catholics in the Philippines since about 1540 I think."

"What on earth are you blethering on about. What has that to do with Danny's girl?"

"Just that I've seen her in Church. She's Catholic and got Danny taking instruction by the looks of it. Watch it, if your jaw drops any lower you'll need a construction crew of navvies to lift it."

"But Danny never said –"

"Did you give him time to say anything? For God's sake, woman, the girl's a stranger in a strange land with no family round her – just as you once were. She seems a decent wee body."

"Have you spoken to her?"

"No, she doesn't speak to strange men – not like some I could mention. I saw her with Danny. Want me to find out their address?"

"What for?"

"She's your daughter-in-law and from the looks of her it won't be too long before she's the mother of your second grandbairn. At least this one won't be born out of wedlock. God, Kate, you should see your face. You of all people should know how it feels to be alone and friendless surrounded by bigoted, stiff necked Scots. I *will* get their address. It's up to you what you do with it. Now, is there any tea in this house? I'm dying for a cup."

"Terence O'Neil, you can't just duck out of an argument like that —"

"I wasn't aware we were having an argument."

"Just how long have you known about Danny's wife?"

Terence shrugged. "Two, maybe three weeks."

"And you said nothing to me!"

"It was hardly up to me to say anything. It was Danny's business. I thought that was what he was going to tell you the night I met him at Granny's."

"Well, he didn't. He got off on something quite different … and we quarrelled."

Kate did make some tea but the atmosphere remained tense with Kate continually going back to her misjudgement of Jenny and the gossip in Govan about Danny. Finally Terence left early.

Chapter 14

Granny Gorbals was in a high old state of excitement and indeed had been dithering about in this way for days past.

It was the promise of a 'wee night' at Jumble Jean's at last, which had produced such a state, and from early morning on the appointed day she had been hard at work baking some of her famous sponge cakes so that she would be well equipped to take with her the traditional and normally expected 'wee minding' to her hostess. When she came into Kate's flat for her daily darg of looking after Hannah she said: "Right, Kate, that's my baking finished for tonight. And, of course, I've brought in a wee bit tasting for Hannah."

Hannah was quick to show that not only did she understand what Granny had said but, in smacking her lips noisily in anticipation, she was sharing her future enjoyment of the promised treat with her nearest and dearest.

Kate smiled happily when Granny enfolded Hannah in a bearhug. Drawing her shawl round her shoulders she turned. "That's me off to my work ... and you folks can get a bit of peace and quiet to carry on with your two handed eating."

Granny and Hannah grinned in unison.

"All right. Talk about here's your hat what's your hurry? Anyway Granny, about tonight; young Mrs Adams from your church has promised to sit in with Hannah and tell her stories, if Hannah's a good girl."

This brought a chorus of, "Hannah's a good girl," which sped Kate on her way.

The rain nearly soaked Kate and Granny as they made their way to Jumble Jean's nearby tenement, so the warm welcome was doubly appreciated. Jean hustled them out of the dank night air into her gas-lit single end with a fire roaring up the chimney.

The formalities of tea, scones, and, of course, Granny's cream sponges safely over, Granny who – had been on her best pinkie-cocking behaviour in the imagined style of a lady of quality sipping tea – visibly relaxed.

Jean, having ensured that her guests were comfortably ensconced on either side of the fire, said: "Kate, remember that night we had the lecture from that bore who ended his Temperance Lecture with some stories about the Humours of the Kirk?"

Kate nodded. "I told you about some of them didn't I, Granny? Did I tell you about the time a minister inquired after a dying woman only to be told: 'Dinnae fash yersel meenister, Aunt Lizzie's no deed jist yet, but we've got the whisky in for the funeral.'"

Granny cackled. "No, but did ye ever hear about the man at a funeral that none of the other mourners knew, who, after everyone had had a good drink in them, admitted he hadn't known the deceased at all, but his own doctor had recommended a wee outing to cheer him up and 'What better to lift the spirits than a good going Scottish funeral tea – except maybe an Irish wake.'"

"Aye," Jean said, "wakes and funeral teas might give people a laugh but sermons can be gey dreich things. Most congregations hate to have the minister read his sermon. In one I heard of, the minister had his sermon all divided into topics on separate sheets of paper and when he came to 'Hope and Charity' he stopped and scrabbled among his papers. A voice from the body of the kirk called out: 'Dinnae waste yer time looking fur yer wee bit paper, meenister. "Hope and Charity" went fleeing oot yon windae hauf an oor or mair since.'"

Kate and Granny laughed and Jean went on: "Another story on reading the sermon has one auld biddy, when asked by the minister if she had enjoyed the sermon, thinking for a minute before saying: 'There were three faults, minister: one, it was read; two it was badly read; and three it wisnae worth reading in the first place.'

"But not all the stories are about sermons being read, one Beadle was asked how a new Minister was settling in said: 'It's no easy tae say. Ye see it's gey seldom we get any sicht o him. Six days o the week he's invisible, then on the Sabbath he's incomprehensible.'"

"Have you no stories, Kate?" Jean asked.

"Once, when Pearce managed to persuade me to go with him to his High Anglican service, the priest glared down at the congregation just after the collection has been made. 'When I look at the congregation I ask myself, 'where are the poor?' But when I look at the collection I ask 'Where are the rich?'

"I remember when I was a girl, before my father died, at one of his services – he was a lay preacher – he told one man who seemed to be falling asleep to take some snuff. Everyone laughed – except my father – when the man said: 'Put some snuff in the sermon!'"

"My word, Kate. And that was grand, just grand. Nothing like a good laugh, is there? Ah'm sure nothing like that ever happened in my religion ... we've got too much respect for our clergy. Humours of the Priests? Hmph, somehow Ah don't think so. Though having said that, old Father Casey can give a real belter of a story, especially when he's been a guest at the celebration party for a Christening.

"At one party he told us a story about a priest and a minister who had gambled away the parish funds. Desperate to make up their losses, they decided on one last gamble. Having placed their bets, they sat together in the priest's house.

"'Our father who art in heaven make it come in at a hundred to seven,' the minister prayed.

"'Hail Mary, full of grace, please make our horse win the race,' the priest said.

"Just at that moment there was a thunderous knock at the front door. Both looked at it wide eyed but before they could move, a loud voice said: 'This here's the Holy Ghost Ah've bin sent tae say yer horse has loast.'"

Chapter 15

Kate sighed as she looked down at a fitfully sleeping Hannah. Somehow, the older Hannah grew, the noisier, more disruptive and more disturbed she became. Certainly, Granny Gorbals acted as her minder when Kate was out working, but now with Granny herself at seventy-five beginning to show her advanced age, and with Jenny departed, God knows where, matters were fast approaching a crisis point. Kate chewed at her lower lip as she mentally debated what was to be done. Of one thing she was sure, something had to be resolved and the sooner the better. It was becoming abundantly clear with each returning day that not only was Hannah becoming a bigger problem, she was also a burden for life. Kate shook her head as she mentally chastised herself for thinking this way. She would be the first to admit that poor Hannah was the most loving of God's creatures and was the most appreciative of cuddles, kisses, and any and all of the many little treats which came her way.

Yes, thought Kate. *That is all very fine on a day-to-day basis, but what of the long term future? What in God's name did that hold for Hannah once I've departed this life? There would be no Jenny to pick up the pieces. Granny Gorbals, in the natural progression of life and death, would be long gone; and as for Danny, my beloved Danny Boy ... what of him?*

Kate pursed her lips at the very thought of his name. *Of course, I would always love him, but I know now that Danny had his own major problem – openly living in Scotland with his Filipino wife.*

Weren't there enough bonnie Scottish lassies for him to have chosen a suitable bride from among their ranks? Or what about an Irish Colleen? But no! What on earth had possessed the lad? The idiot boy had had to get himself involved with a Filipino girl while on his travels abroad. According to the Govan gossip, Danny had a near-murderous punch-up with her brothers; and was then frog-marched to the nearest temple or whatever passed in that foreign land for God's house – no, that couldn't be right: Terence said she was Catholic – there to make an honest woman of her in the hastily arranged marriage ceremony

And if he had thought all that bad enough, it was as nothing compared to the Scottish scenario. Apart from the Coolies who regularly came and went from their far travelled ships in the various Glasgow docks, hardly any Scot had ever before seen such a foreigner. And now to have one actually living in their midst in a mixed marriage! The only other mixed marriages in the area were those between Roman Catholics and Protestants ... and heaven alone knew how much trouble they caused between nosy neighbours, so-called do-gooders and interfering relatives. If she was Catholic as Terence said and Danny Protestant then they had that hurdle too.

Kate's thoughts froze at that point. Her mind had glossed over the rest of what Terence had said in his lecture about her lack of charity.

Terence was Catholic! She'd never thought of that. So she and Terence might well have the same troubles. *I'll not think of that right now. I'll cross that bridge when and if I come to it.*

Kate came out of her reverie with a start when she heard the cheery voice of Granny Gorbals from the hallway. It would never do to let Granny know of the worries and the dark secrets she now harboured in relation to her family. But it would have taken a better actress than Kate Kinnon to hoodwink old Granny. Settling her bulk in the Master's chair, Granny folded her arms across her chest. "Right then, Kate Kinnon. So what ails you now, my friend?"

Despite herself, Kate could not hold back a smile at Granny's usual direct, no-nonsense approach.

"You're right, as ever, Granny. It seems there's always some problem these days."

Although Granny nodded, thus encouraging Kate to go on, there was a second's hesitation as Kate debated in her mind exactly how much she could safely tell the old woman. After all, with Granny's strict moral code, religious observance, and hidebound ideas, she would be scandalised to learn of Danny's totally bizarre living arrangements. Thus decided, Kate gave a nod of determination and opted instead to get another, totally different family worry off her chest.

"Well, Granny, dear, it's like this. I've been sitting here worrying myself into a decline over what's to happen to poor Hannah."

Granny's rheumy eyes widened in amazement.

''What rubbish are you talking now, Kate? What's to happen to Hannah is what happens to her every day in life. I'll be looking after her."

Kate smiled at the absurdity of it all.

"Uch, Granny, I don't mean today. I'm talking about the future … I mean a time when neither you nor I are … not to put too fine a point on it … well … when we are –"

"Kate Kinnon. Will you stop your havering? You mean when we are both dead and buried. Right?"

Kate nodded and Granny went on: "Suppose we worry about that when the time comes? Mind you, once the coffin lid closes over us, we'll not be able to worry anyway. But meanwhile, let's stick with the idea of one day at a time. And just you remember this, my girl, as long as there's breath in my body I'll be looking after the dear wee soul. She's more precious to me than any of my far-flung so-called family. I just fair love that dear wee lassie. And she knows it. Look how she can twist me round her wee finger."

The emotions that surged through Kate at these words left her feeling choked to the point where it was all she could do to nod feebly. But if Kate was struck dumb, the same could not be said for her old friend and neighbour. Rubbing her hands in anticipation, she gave a cackle of childlike glee and said: "Now then, my lass, we're not at our funeral tea just yet and don't forget; we'll be the ones missing out on any jollifications that day. So did I guess rightly that you perhaps were just about to mention a wee pot of our own special Candleriggs brew?"

Kate laughed delightedly at Granny's childlike exuberance.

"Trust you Granny to think that one out. I must say, it had never crossed my mind to think that at our wake everybody else would be getting tore into the whisky and the sweet sherry. Aye, you're right, why don't we make up for it now."

So saying – and with the problem of what to do with Hannah, not so much solved, as shelved by Granny – Kate searched out the medicinal bottle of whisky from its hiding place.

Later that same evening as she prepared Hannah for bed, Kate got down on her knees and said a hearty prayer to the Almighty. She thanked him that they had got through yet another day without injury, undue incident or even too horrendous a battle of wills.

Kate's last thought before her head touched the pillow: *One day at a time, Sweet Jesus. Maybe Granny with her words of wisdom and the teachings of the Good Book were right after all. True, they had shelved the matter of Hannah's uncertain future. As for Danny and his unsuitable choice of a wife ... well tomorrow was another day, time enough to worry herself about that then. In any case, for all anyone knew, she might well be a perfectly nice girl, as Terence has said. And if that was the case, the poor lass would find the racial and religious bigotry in Glasgow even harder to deal with. For the poor Filipino girl, as Danny's wife living in Scotland, her life would be one long uphill struggle. And heaven help any bairns from their union, for that was the reality in narrow minded Scotland.*

Chapter 16

Glasgow Fair Friday was only two day's away and with it Kate's last pay poke from Mac's Restaurant for two weeks. Two weeks of unpaid holiday at a time when Kate most needed to keep herself busy, to keep her mind from brooding over the Kinnon family's fateful trip 'Doon the watter' to Royal Rothesay. The tragedy of Isabella's drowning, the death of what had promised to be a happy reconciliation between Kate and Pearce, the beginning of the downward spiral for Pearce into despair, depression, and the bitter, angry man he became.

Kate sighed as she rode the top deck of the tram, for once reluctant to put pencil to paper. Then she shook herself.

I'll walk up to Terence's barrow and make up with him. It's not right that we should fall out because Danny's made a fool of himself. Terence was just speaking his mind – even if he was wrong.

But there was no sign of Terence at the barrow. Instead, Auld Shuggie stood scratching his head under his bunnet.

"Oh, it's yersel, Kate Mavourneen. Sure, wasn't the bold Terence just after talking about ye."

"Aye, Shuggie. When will himself be back?"

"I dinnae rightly ken. A fortnight mibbe? Ah'm tae look after the barrow for the Fair Fortnight."

Kate felt abandoned.

"Here, Kate, lassie. Yer no gonnae faint or anything like that ur ye? Ah telt ye wance afore it's very bad fur business – folks might think it's because o' ma prices."

Kate smiled at his joke. "What did Terence have to say about me?"

"When?"

"Just now, you said Terence had been talking about me."

"Oh, aye. He said ye needit a holiday. Someplace away frae Glesga. That ye were looking fair wabit."

"Thanks, Shuggie. That's really cheered me up. How the hell can I afford a holiday? I've got two weeks without a pay poke."

Shuggie shuffled, took off his bunnet to scratch his head, and finally blew his nose heartily into a not too clean rag. Looking down, he cleared his throat.

"Terence said if ye wernae sae stiff-necked prideful and bloody concerned aboot what people would think, ye could be real comfortable with him."

Kate felt her face flush.

"Sorry, Kate, lass, but ye did ask what Terence said and that's the honest truth. That's what he said. And if ye want ma advice –"

"I don't."

"Well, Ah'll gie it tae ye anyway, it's fur free. Ye'll never get another man as good as Terence. Don't let him slip through yer fingers fur fear o what folks will say. Tae hell wi them; it's *yer* life."

Kate turned away and started the walk home to Candleriggs.

Late that evening Kate sat at home concerned that she hadn't been able to make up with Terence after their row about Danny's wife and Terence's silly lecture. She brooded on the prospect of two weeks without a farthing coming in since Mac's Restaurant would be closed for the Fair Fortnight. Her worried thoughts were interrupted by a knock on her door and Kate rushed to answer, sure that it would be Terence with a peace offering. Despite her disappointment, Kate, ever the caring hostess, welcomed Shuggie as he stood clutching his ancient tweed bunnet.

"Come on in, Shuggie. What on earth brings you out to this end of the Candleriggs on such a night of pouring rain? Come on, come in."

Shuggie only twisted his bunnet between his hands and shook his head. A waft of whisky fumes accompanied his words.

"Naw, naw, Mistress Kinnon, Ah'll no come in drip aw ower yer clean floor – if it's aw the same tae ye. Terence said Ah wis jist tae deliver his message then get tae Hell oot o it."

Despite herself, Kate's spirits rose. "Oh! What message would that be?"

Delving into an inner fold of his wringing wet, moth-eaten jacket Shuggie pulled out a bulky envelope which he thrust into Kate's hand, turned, and fled.

Kate called after him: "At least pop in for a cup of tea," but she realised she was wasting her breath. It was the lure of a much stronger beverage than weak tea that called him to calm his nerves – whatever was causing his unusual anxiety.

Although intrigued to find out what was in the fat envelope – surely more than a simple letter of apology – Kate first looked in on Hannah, then mug of tea to hand she prised open the package. She frowned, puzzled, as a second smaller envelope thudded to the kitchen table.

She read Terence's letter through twice before finally daring to open the second envelope. Her fingers trembled as she handled its contents – it was a dream come true. In an agony of indecision she pondered: *Should she disturb Granny Gorbals at this late hour? No, the news could wait till morning. She would savour it to herself till then. Granny is never going to believe this, not in a month of Sundays.*

Next morning, seated before Kate's roaring fire, with a generous helping of porridge inside her, Granny beamed in delight and appreciation.

"Kate, lass, it was awfie good o ye tae have me in for breakfast. But listen, there was no need to be wasting coal on a July morning just for me."

"Granny, if you can tell me the secret of making a pot of porridge on an dead fire that would be just grand. Anyway July or not, it's still pouring with rain, and raw and miserable with it. So we might as well be comfortable. Forebye a cheery fire's as good a way to celebrate as any, is that not so?"

"Celebrate? Celebrate, ye say? Ye've no money coming in for a fortnight soon, ye've had a row with Terence, and yer haverin' on about celebratin'. Kate lass, has all the stramash addled yer brain?"

Kate laughed. "No, Granny. There is something to celebrate. I've had a letter from Terence. He's well, but he's gone off somewhere. Before he left, he sent Shuggie round last night with a letter and a present. The dear, good, wonderful man, he's sent us return boat tickets – cabin class no less – to Ireland. One each for you, me, and Hannah. We're to have the rent-free run of a wee cottage in Ballygally – it belongs to some old landlord he knows. A friend of a friend will meet us off the boat – an estate worker name of Anthony – with a jaunting cart to escort us in style. We're all going to our beloved Ireland for the Fair Fortnight!"

The holiday in Ireland was all, and more than Kate and Granny could ever have hoped for in their wildest flights of imagination. They had travelled like ladies of quality all the way, and the estate hand, Anthony, had as promised met them off the boat.

At the cottage Anthony's wife, Bernadette, had a real Irish welcome waiting for them. Later, stuffed to capacity with a massive helping of stew, soda bread, and potato cakes, Kate and

Granny grinned at each other. Almost as if it was an effort to speak, Granny had finally broken the companionable silence. "Well now, Kate. Is this not just grand?"

And grand was exactly what it turned out to be. As each idyllic day followed another, Bernadette arrived at the cottage to cook, clean, and generally look after 'her ladies'.

Although prone to blether, there was one topic on which Bernadette was tight lipped. Each time Kate expressed a wish to call on the lady at the big house to thank her for her generosity in letting them use the cottage, the otherwise garrulous Bernadette muttered: "No need, no need at all. Anyway she's old. She doesn't receive visitors."

And there the matter had to rest until, towards the end of the holiday, Kate tried to insist on her wish to thank their benefactress.

Bernadette flushed and snapped: "Mistress Kinnon, leave it! Once and for all, forget her mightiness up at the big house. Truth is, she doesn't even know you're here. She lets her son have the run of the place. He travels a lot. His friends come and go at their own convenience, and as you've seen Anthony and I look after his guests."

Fancy Terence having a friend in such high places as the lady of the manor's son, Kate thought. *Aye, a strange world indeed.*

When the last day of their dream holiday arrived, it wasn't only Hannah who was in tears as they waved goodbye. Even so Hannah was the most upset, for not only had she been spoiled, petted, and pampered by the kindly Irish couple but she had to part with her friend, the pony Peggy.

Back in the Second City of the Empire, life resumed its familiar routine. Kate, still in a glow of happiness from her holiday, was shopping in the Saltmarket in something of a daze when she heard two gossiping women mention the name, 'that Mistress Kinnon'. Dawdling over her choice of quarter cabbages from the kerbside display she strained to hear what was being said about her, but all she could make out was: "... aye, no wonder he sent her packing, ... off to Ireland ... left him free to lust after the other one ..."

At that, one of the shawlie women glanced up and, catching sight of Kate at the vegetable stall, nudged her friend and they bustled off, leaving Kate frowning in bewilderment.

Now, what was that all about? It's a puzzle, but I'm damn sure I'll make it my business to find out the answer.

Abruptly shaken out of her reverie of happy memories of the holiday in Ireland, Kate set off with a new determination in her step. *If there was one person in the Candleriggs who could tell all I need to know about Terence and about any gossip going round, it was Auld Shuggie. Finding him could be tricky, since he frequented several different drinking howffs, but find him I will.*

For three days after hearing that scrap of gossip, Kate kept her eyes and ears wide open, but she heard nothing else and there was no sign of Shuggie. However, from the many meaningful looks and thumbs jerked in her direction she was aware she was still the subject of whatever scandalous gossip that was being traded round the Saltmarket and Candleriggs.

Kate rounded a corner into Virginia Street and there was Shuggie. As Kate advanced on him Shuggie looked around him like a cornered animal desperate for some way out. Hampered as he clearly was by the amount of whisky he had taken on board, short of collapsing at her feet in an alcoholic haze, there was no escape. Drunk or not, Shuggie was still sufficiently alert to recognise a determined Kate Kinnon when he saw her.

"Right now, Shuggie. The very man. If anybody has answers it's you. So get talking."

Shuggie staggered back from her and, seeking a life line, lurched towards the nearest lamp post. Kate waited with what patience she could muster until he was safely tethered.

"You were the messenger with those Irish boat tickets. So you must know – is it true? Did Terence want me out of the way so that he could go lusting after some other woman? Some woman to satisfy his manly needs since I won't wed him or lie with him till after my proper days of mourning. Was that his grand scheme?"

Shuggie gasped. "Och, Kate, lass, it's no fitting for a decent widow woman like yersel tae talk o such things. Ah'm no Terence's keeper. Ah cannae read his mind. Aw Ah ken is that he thought ye needed a holiday and that he had some private business he wanted tae dae while ye were no in Glasgow."

Kate took a step closer. "I can imagine what private business he had. It's true then. He did go rollicking off after some other woman. No wonder I'm the talk of the neighbourhood. Oh, the shame of it!"

"Ah didnae say that, Kate—"

"Next time you see yon woman-hungry Irishman tell him ... tell him ... uch damn it all ... tell him I never want to see him again. You got it, Shuggie? Tell him to go to Hell!"

Kate turned and strode off and didn't hear Shuggie mutter: "Ah didnae say he's aff after another woman, did Ah? How the hell am Ah supposed tae ken what he was up tae?"

Chapter 17

The month of August had come and gone and the glorious holiday in Ireland was now nothing more than a memory. Of Terence there had been neither sight nor sound, so Kate presumed that Shuggie, drunk or not, had somehow delivered her message – terse, rude, and unforgettable as it was. A knock on the door roused Kate from her dark thoughts and introspection. She gasped in amazement at the sight that greeted her when she opened the door. The smartly dressed young woman who stood on the landing awaiting admittance bore no resemblance to the sometime pathetic, dishevelled drunk of former days.

She invited Jenny and Theresa in and Jenny said: "Mammy, it's like a dream come true. Coming back like this to see you again. I'd never have had the courage to return after the dreadful rows we had, but it's all thanks to Terence."

At the very mention of his name Kate frowned. "Oh, Terence is it? And how, may I ask, does he come into the picture?"

If Jenny sensed the anger behind her mother's words, and the atmosphere, she gave no sign. Instead, she settled herself comfortably in her chair, then quietly and calmly told her story.

Kate, already bursting with questions, listened with what patience she could muster. When Jenny finished speaking, there was a silence that could be felt. Kate's lips were pressed into a thin, taut line, around the edges of which was a rim of white.

At last, Kate said: "Right, Jenny, let me get this straight. You say you were working in a guest house in, of all places, Rothesay?"

"I know it seems strange. And to tell you the truth, I could hardly bear to go back there to the Island of Bute ... where Isabella drowned –"

"So why did you?' Kate interrupted.

"Well, that time when I left here ... I was desperate ... especially with wee Theresa to care for. I just didn't know what to do or even where to go. Then I remembered Mrs Graham's lovely guest house. She was so nice to me after Dadda smashed my doll. She hugged me and said it was Dadda she was angry with and that I was to remember that if ever I needed help."

Kate gasped in astonishment. "I don't remember any of that. But you actually got work there? If I remember Mrs Graham aright, that good lady would have no truck with the Demon Drink ... so you must have sobered up pretty quickly."

"As I told you that night we quarrelled, I'd been off the drink, or had been trying not to drink for a while. I just had enough in my purse for the fare to Rothesay. I hadn't thought past that, but I was stone cold sober with not even a whiff of alcohol when I spoke to Mrs Graham."

Kate took a deep breath, she was longing to ask the question but dreading the answer.

"And Terence? What precisely was his part in your great adventure?"

At the mention of his name Jenny's face softened.

"Mammy, that's the marvellous wonder of it all. During the Glasgow Fair he came looking for me! How he knew I was in Rothesay I'll never know, but wasn't it wonderful? He actually came looking for me. Can you credit that?"

Kate swallowed hard. *Yes I could credit it – the gossips had been right. Terence O'Neil has sent me off to Ireland, out of the way, so that 'he could go lusting after some other woman.'*

The fact that the other woman was her own daughter made it all the harder to bear.

With her mind buzzing over and over again with the words, 'Terence came looking for me,' Kate was only dimly aware of Jenny babbling on almost non-stop as she sought to bring her Mammy up to date on recent events. With her head bursting and a sinking feeling in her stomach, Kate felt Jenny might as well be talking in a foreign language.

After a sleepless night of tossing and turning, Kate felt she would scream when, at breakfast, Jenny again started chattering nineteen to the dozen. However, by her second cup of tea she made a determined effort to concentrate on what Jenny was saying. No sooner had she mentally sat up and paid attention than she stopped Jenny in mid-sentence.

"Who did you say has helped you beat the Demon Drink?"

"Mammy! Have you listened to nothing I've told you? I told you all about Hamish and me last night. Honestly, I gave it to you chapter and verse."

"And who might Hamish be when he's at home? For God's sake, Jenny, you don't change do you? Is one man never enough for you?"

Jenny frowned. "Listen, Mammy. Is that not exactly what I'm telling you? What I've been trying to tell you since last night. Hamish and me ... well ... we're engaged. And he's willing to take on wee Theresa as well. He's good with her. He's a real decent man, a hard worker with a good job at the tweed mill –"

"But Terence? What about him? According to you he'd been combing the country looking for you."

Jenny gave a tut of annoyance.

"Are you completely away with the fairies? Yes, Terence was determined to find me ... but for you! It was all for your sake. So that you and I could make up our differences. Right? Have you got it clear in your head now?"

Kate sat open-mouthed and soundless. Jenny rose, walked

round the table and put her arms round her mother.

"One way and another, once your official year and a day of mourning is past, one thing is sure, it looks as though you've found yourself a good man as well. Like me and Hamish, I mean."

Looking up through her tears, Kate said: "Oh, and how do you come the that conclusion, Miss Know-it-all?"

"Think about it, for goodness's sake. It seems perfectly clear to me that Terence wants only the best, the very best, for you. That's why he packed you off to that estate in Ireland for a wee holiday. While you were out of the country he put his time to good use. For it's up to him and him alone that you and I are no longer at loggerheads."

Kate grasped Jenny's hand with a grip that made her knuckles show white. Jenny finally eased her hand free.

"Now then, how about a fresh brewing of tea to celebrate? After all, it's not every day you have the return of the prodigal daughter and a bit of good news into the bargain."

Good news, Kate thought. *Oh, Jenny lass, if only you knew. If only you knew how in my heart and with my evil thoughts I have wronged Terence. My fine, caring, handsome Terence. I've sent him a message via the good, if inebriated, offices of Shuggie to say that I never, ever, want to see him again. Dear God! What a fool, an utter fool, I've been. Will nothing in this life ever go right for me?"*

Even the mug of sweet tea Jenny gave her did nothing to take away the sour taste of bile in her mouth.

Chapter 18

As Granny came into Kate's home she seemed less than her usual cheery self. In answer to Kate's concerned query, the old woman hastened to reassure her friend she was perfectly all right, in fact, never better.

There was a silence between them and, as Kate studied the old woman's face, she was alarmed to see Granny's lips tremble, an unusual sign of weakness in this hardy old lady. Kate laid a hand on Granny's arm.

"Right, Granny, come on, let's be having no more of this nonsense."

With an effort, Granny seemed to gather her inner resources until finally she said: "Cannae hide anything from you, Kate, noo can Ah?"

Kate smiled. The old woman's speech, despite her long year of self imposed exile from her beloved Emerald Isle, was still a weird mixture of the gutteral harshness of Glasgow patter and the softer strains of the Ireland of blessed memory. As if talking to a shy child, Kate coaxed: "Come on now, Granny, you might as well tell me, whatever it is, for you know in your old bones, I'll wheedle it out of you in the long run. Anyway, would you be thinking now, would mibbe a fresh brewing of tea help matters along?"

But even before the proffered mug of sweet tea was being raised to her lips, Granny sighed. "It's that Mistress Buchan."

Kate frowned. "Can't say I know her. Anyway, who's she when she's at home? And what on earth has she done to upset you this way?

Granny took a long slug of her tea. Then, with great precision, she laid it down on the creepie stool by the hearth.

"No, you wouldn't know her, Kate. At least not yet! But you mark my words, the auld besom will very soon make her mark."

With Kate still frowning in bewilderment. Granny launched into her tale. It seemed that the aforementioned Mrs Buchan was already known locally – infamous, in fact – to many who had suffered years of misery at her hands, in her self-appointed role as Queen of the Close. While she had stayed in her close in the Saltmarket, safely distant from Granny and Kate, that was one thing. But now, with rent Quarter Day fast approaching, local rumour was rampant that the martinet would be getting the key and then flitting into a single-end on the ground floor of Granny's close. On hearing this, Kate began to see a chink of light. For Irish exile as she herself was, even Kate had lived long enough in Glasgow and its tenements to know something of its social structure.

From her own work in the posh, upmarket, wally closes round at Mrs Scott's, she knew enough to keep well out of the way of the Queen of the Close of that particular building. The guardian of the common entrance there not only ruled her subjects with an iron hand, minus any velvet glove, but invariably each time Kate appeared to do Mrs Scott's housework, the grand dame, strong madam, call her what you will, was always on hand to greet Kate with a fishlike gaze and sharply spoken orders to take extra care not only with the door appointments but also with the high standards adhered to in 'my close'.

Yes, living in a Glasgow tenement meant many things, not least that to reach one's home, it was necessary to walk through the common entrance, known to all and sundry as The Close. No matter what assortment of characters each building contained, be they clean, honest, God-fearing families, or those of the 'durty wee midden' variety, nevertheless every close had one ... a Queen of the Close!

This unique phenomenon was a self-appointed position and one of great prestige, authority, and importance. The Queen of the Close took it upon herself and her broad shoulders: to prevent legless drunks from using the common entrance either as an open-air, draughty cludgie, or as convenient doss-house; to check or otherwise castigate cheeky, unruly children; to scare off stray cats and dogs and prevent them from bespoiling the doorsteps and coconut mats of proud, hardworking Scottish housewives; to see that the rota of stair-washing was strictly adhered to; to sweep into the back-court middens the previous night's accumulation of fish-and-chip newspapers and other even more unsavoury rubbish; to ensure that the pipe-clayed ornate pattern always so lovingly and expertly executed around the perimeter of the close was kept looking pristine; to see to it that no housewife ever had the audacity to jump the queue in the oft-disputed matter of who's turn it was to 'hing oot the washin' in the back-court; and at all times to keep a weather-eye on the comings and goings of all visitors, uninvited hawkers, scum and other such unauthorised personnel to the building.

So, dragging her thoughts away from the confrontations she had coped with at Mrs Scott's close, Kate with a puzzled frown gazed at Granny.

"Yes, Granny, I begin to see what you mean. And believe me, I've met many a high and mighty specimen in the West End with their tiled, wally closes and their stuck-up attitude. But let's face it, surely it's different in the Candleriggs. And you and me, we've always got on fine with Mrs McGarrigle, our own Queen of the Close. We've never really had a cross word with her, now have we?"

Granny stared at Kate, as though seeing for the first time a rather wandered wean and one who wasn't quite the full twenty shillings in the pound.

"Kate, lass. The names. Think aboot it, the names. Of course we aye got on jist grand with Mrs McGarrigle. But dinnae forget she was from the Emerald Isle, just like us."

Beginning to see where all this was heading, Kate waited for Granny to continue.

"Aye, that Mrs McGarrigle, she was one thing. But see that Mistress Buchan … she's Scottish, strict Presbyterian to her fingertips – Ah'll bet that never a dribble of doctored tea ever passes her tightly pursed lips, but above all else, Kate – and listen weel tae this, my lass – that woman hates the Irish. Aye, hates every fibre of our being. She absolutely loathes the Irish, our speech, our customs, in fact every bloody thing the Irish are, or ever will be."

Kate nodded in understanding, for it was a measure of Granny's concern that she had chosen to swear. Leaning forward, Kate took Granny's hands in hers.

"Listen, my old friend, the infamous Mrs Buchan might be all that you say, and mibbe even more for all I know, but one thing's sure …"

Granny waited for Kate to go on.

"Auld besom, she might be. But you and me, Granny, we're a match for anybody. In fact, we could take on the Devil, aye Auld Nick himself. Mind you, for all we got on so well with Mrs McGarrigle, do you mind in her early days here when she was trying to make her mark as Queen of the Close? Do you remember how she got her come-uppence from us?"

At the memory of how Granny had given the woman the edge of her tongue when the ill-informed Mrs McGarrigle had tried to upbraid Saft Sandy, both Kate and Granny burst out laughing.

"Oh, aye, it was a red-letter day that one. Poor Saft Sandy didnae know any better. And some big bully boy had telt him tae stick a Bible tract through Mrs McGarrigle's letter box. What the bad boy hadnae telt Sandy was that he'd wrote in a whole lot of swear words, albeit misspelt but clear enough for her to get the message. Then Sandy's sticky fingers left their imprint over her polished brass letterbox and she grabbed him by the scruff of the neck. Near aff her heid wi it all, Mrs McGarrigle was readin' him the riot act."

"But you told her, Granny. Told her that saft in the heid or not, poor Sandy was still one of God's creatures and you would never allow a word against him, far less a cuff on the ears. You're a star, Granny, an angel in disguise. And there's only ever been or will be one Queen of this close for me – you."

Chapter 19

The moment Kate got out of bed that morning, she felt that nothing would go right for her that day. It wasn't just Hannah's screams – more horrendous than usual – which made her feel so. No, she had awoken to a dream of being in the cool, clean air of a remote farm in her beloved Ireland, a cottage just like the one they stayed at in Glasgow Fair fortnight.

She managed to get herself energised enough to start her day with that first essential – a cup of hot tea. While the kettle was coming to the boil she did her best to placate Hannah with soothing noises, gentle cuddles, and the lilting air of a distantly remembered Irish lullaby.

The rattle of the letter box disturbed her moment of peace with the tea in front of the fire. A brown envelope lay on the hall floor and Kate stared at it. It looked official somehow, the kind of envelope bills arrived in, but she couldn't think of any outstanding bills other than the account 'on the slate' at the corner shop, and they certainly wouldn't waste the money on a stamp.

When she finally opened the letter she had to read it twice – a rent increase!

Her first thought was for her old friend across the landing: *How in God's name will Granny ever be able to pay such a king's ransom?*

The minute Granny Gorbals arrived to care for Hannah it was

immediately obvious she too had received the dreaded letter. Without even waiting for the ritual cup of tea, Granny blurted out: "Oh, Kate! An extra sixpence a week. They might as well have said a hundred pounds and be done with it. Where on earth are we two widow women to find extra bawbees like that?"

It took all of Kate's diplomacy, tact, and caring attitude to calm Granny down to the point where the two friends could discuss their latest financial disaster with a modicum of common sense. Every bit as aggrieved as Granny, Kate voiced the opinion of both when she said: "Wouldn't you have thought they could have found a less sneaky way of going about things?"

Granny sucked the air through the gravestones of her teeth, only then nodding sagely and saying: "Aye. You speak true, Katy, my lass. If there had to be a rent increase – and God knows those landlords are filthy rich already – surely the rent collector could have told us in person when he comes as usual on Friday?"

Kate nodded her head. "You're right. There was no need for a big official letter, fit to put the fear of God in us. Finding the rent money is already enough of a nightmare without that. And as for another silver sixpence every week …"

Kate's words trailed off, leaving hanging in the air between them an almost tangible bridge of misery.

Later that same morning as Kate trudged along the Saltmarket, the burden of financial near-ruin weighed heavily. What on earth was she to do? How could she possibly help Granny Gorbals? One thing was abundantly clear; Granny's meagre finances were already stretched to the limit. The fiercely independent old woman had firmly but politely turned down Kate's suggestion that perhaps she could squash into the Kinnon household, given that she was in Kate's flat every day anyway when she looked after Hannah.

Independent to the last, Granny had stoutly declared: "You mean it kindly, Kate. I realise that. But we both know it just wouldn't work."

And there the matter had rested, with Granny having the last word. "If that extra sixpence a week is beyond my means, there's only one thing for met. And that's Merryflats."

At the very mention of the dreaded and ridiculously misnamed workhouse, Granny's eyes had filled with tears. Kate, having once seen the gaunt grey buildings over in Govan, and knowing full well the only way any pauper ever came out of there was in a coffin, she too found herself dabbing frantically at a cascade of tears.

Even now, amid the hustle and bustle of the Saltmarket, Kate's eyes kept filling to point where she could hardly see to keep moving along the crowded street. At last she stopped in front of a large building, pulled out from her pocket the rag that did duty as a handkerchief, and wiped away her tears.

Giving herself a mental shake, she thought: *Right then, Kate Kinnon. No more of this nonsense. You'll never help Granny or yourself this way.*

About to move further along the street, Kate suddenly saw a notice pinned to the door of the building. And for no other reason than to take her mind off her worries, she started to read it. At the foot of the given details, printed in heavy black lettering which seemed almost to jump off the page at her, were the words: ONLY IRISH NEED APPLY.

On seeing this, Kate laughed aloud and clapped her hands in delight, as she thought: *Surely someone with a sense of humour there! A far cry indeed from the days when Pearce and I first came to Glasgow. Then it was a case of every notice regarding job applications, or the renting of derelict yet overpriced rooms, bearing the banner heading: NO IRISH NEED APPLY.*

Still chuckling, Kate set off again, determined to get a nice bit of fish as a wee treat for Granny's tea. Halfway along the pavement, Kate stopped in her tracks so abruptly that a workman close on her heels all but cannoned into her. Not about to let a mere shawlie woman impede his manly progress in this way, he shook a bunched fist at her and bawled out: "For fuck's sake, Missus. Were ye born daft? Or are ye jist plain knocked stupid wi' cheap booze? One mair meenft and this can o paraffin would hae been cowped aw ower the baith o us."

Muttering an apology, Kate turned on her heels and with all possible speed, headed back the way she had just come, the shouts and curses of the still irate paraffin-can bearer still ringing in her ears. With a reborn spring in her step, and a new purpose in her heart, Kate was beyond caring what he or any other bemused bystander thought of her erratic movements. She was determined to read again that notice. And not only read and digest it ... she had already made up her mind to positive action with respect to such an opportunity. If 'only Irish need apply' were in fact to be the role, then surely she herself was the very woman for the job? Come to think of it, Granny Gorbals too was as Irish as the shamrock. This miserable afternoon was about to turn into one great day for the Irish!

As Kate returned home, she climbed the tenement stairs with all the verve and energy of a much younger woman. Once arrived in the flat, she greeted Granny like a long-lost relative, all the while beaming the smile of victory.

Finally, extricating herself from Kate's bear-hug, Granny leant back, studied Kate's face and said: "Right now. And just what was all that about? For a poor widow woman who trailed out of here this morning looking as if somebody had stole her soda-scone, you've now bounced back grinning from ear to ear ... as if you'd fallen in the Clyde and come up with a gold watch."

Kate laughed in delight both at Granny's look of bemused bewilderment and at the old woman's wonderfully descriptive pictures of Kate's altered mood. Grabbing Granny's hands, Kate said: "No! No gold watch. But Granny, listen to what I have to tell you ... it's something much more fantastic. And it's for both of us. If you agree to fall in with this plan, then we'll have no more talk of Merryflats ... nor of any other workhouse ever again. And we wouldn't have to worry about Mrs Buchan moving in on us as Queen of the Close."

Kate gently guided the old woman to a chair and sat her down.

"I've come across a chance for us that would solve our problems about the rent increase and make a whole new life for us. There's to be a Navvies' Hostel opening near by – a hostel for Irish navvies – and they want Irish women to help run it. If we give up our flats here, we can move into rent-free accommodation at the Navvies' Hostel. We would get free coal and gas in return for me being the cook-cum-housekeeper and for you being the resident caretaker. What do you say, Granny? Will you come in with me for the job? I've got to let them know for sure tomorrow."

Kate stopped, and there was a silence broken only when Granny, having nodded her head vigorously in agreement with all that Kate had suggested, burst into a paroxysm of weeping. At length, she dried her tears and said: "Kate, my darlin girl ... 'twas a God-given day when ye first walked into my life. Ye've brought me more happiness over the years than anyone of my so-called family."

At these words, Kate's own eyes filled with tears. Then, before such strong emotion could engulf her, she summoned a smile and teased Granny with the comment: "And do ye tell me that now auld yin: Just one thing I don't understand. If you're that gloriously happy with life and our proposed new situation, why in God's name are ye still weeping buckets of salt tears?"

With the excitement of the events of the day still surging through her mind, Kate found she could not settle to any of her usual household chores. At one point, she was in half a mind to go across the landing and ask Granny to sit in with Hannah for the rest of the evening, thus freeing Kate to take a wee trip over to Govan to see Betty. Now that Granny had agreed to the exciting new project, Kate felt her own mind would explode if she did not immediately share the secret with somebody ... and what better person then her old friend and confidante, Betty? Kate was still debating whether or not to disturb Granny when she heard someone knocking on her door. When she opened it and saw who it was standing on the mat, Kate let out a squeal of almost girlish delight.

"I don't believe it!"

"Well, Kate, ye'd better believe it and let me in the bloody door before Ah freeze to death out here on the landing. Some welcome this is, Ah must say."

Over the inevitable cup of tea, having given Kate the latest news from Auld Mac's, Betty stared hard at her friend.

"Ah must say, for somebody badly in need of a job, ye're looking hellova pleased with yersel, Kate."

Kate smiled.

"It's true I was gutted when Auld Mac had to let me go in September. But with less business coming in from the yard workers at Fairfields, there was no way he could afford to pay me wages for standing about his kitchen with little or no dishes to wash. But anyway, there was nothing personal about it and it's all in the past now. Today, I've just had the most amazing stroke of luck. Honestly, Betty, you'd never believe it."

"Put it this way, old pal. Ah certainly will never believe it if ye'll not get on and tell me what it is ye're haverin' on about."

Again, Kate told the tale of that morning's mail and of her accidental discovery about the Irish Navvies' Hostel to open in the Saltmarket.

"It was heaven sent, Betty. Granny and I were at our wit's end about the rent increase and out of the blue this happens. We were lucky this day."

"Lucky's no the word for it. It's a bloody miracle, so it is, and Ah wish the pair o' ye aw the best."

Chapter 20

The day of the removal arrived and, game to the last, Auld Shuggie came up trumps yet again as their willing helper. He humped furniture out of both flats, and with the aid of a team of snotty-nosed wee schoolboys, together they somehow manhandled the goods downstairs through the communal close and out to Shuggie's handcart.

Kate had already sent Granny and Hannah on ahead to the new abode with strict instructions to wait in the public seating area of the hostel until such time as Shuggie had arrived and positioned their goods and chattels in their private quarters.

Kate worked away with Shuggie, at the same time, surreptitiously trying to find out from him what news, if any, there might be of Terence.

Eventually, this brought the response: "Oh, Terence, is it? Aye, a real Irish gentleman that one, and no airs or graces or toffee-nosed snootiness about him."

Kate wondered fleetingly if those last words were by way of being a barbed comment about her late, lamented husband. But knowing full well. that over the years of his life Pearce had upset many a common workman by his superior looking-down-his-nose manner, she decided to let it go. Anyway, she was determined to find out all she possibly could about Terence and his current whereabouts. So, taking a deep breath, she again entered the verbal fray.

"Aye, you're right there, Shuggie. In fact we might even call

Terence a scholar and a gentleman. I used to think he had read all yon books on his barrow."

Shuggie laughed in agreement. "That's entirely possible, Mistress Kinnon. For he aye had his head buried in some book or other. But talking of him being a gent ye'll never guess what he did before he left for Ireland that last time."

Kate shook her head and Shuggie went on, enjoying the blether as thoroughly as any sweetwife in her Jenmy-aw-Things shop: "He gave his book barrow to my nephew ... Gave it away, mind you! Didnae sell it. Gave it away lock, stock, and barrow to Dunkie."

At Kate's puzzled look, Shuggie elaborated: "Dunkie. Uch fine well ye ken him ... him wi' the withered arm, nae job, nae trade, nor a hope in Hell o ever getting yin. But for all that, hunners o bootless, half-starved weans aw runnin aboot his single-end. Aye, Terence, God bless him, said it would give Dunkie and his bairns a stake in the future. So, what dae ye' think of that? Am Ah no right? Terence O'Neil, a true Irish gentleman to his very fingertips."

Kate could only nod in silent agreement. If anyone knew what an upright man of honour he was, it was Kate Kinnon. Hadn't he gone off to Ireland on some business or other after he and she had made up following Kate's disastrous misunderstanding over her holiday to Ireland and his search for Jenny? He had said it would give Kate time to reconcile with her daughter and to come to terms with Danny's wife and if possible with Danny himself, as well as allow Kate the proscribed decency of a longer period of mourning for Pearce. Kate would never forget his last words to her before he set off on the Irish boat from the Broomielaw: "Mind now, Kate, you and I have an understanding. I'll be back for you. One fine day, without warning – but probably when you most need the comfort of my arms around you – I'll just turn up on your doorstep. And then, my dearest Kate, then I'll claim you as my bride."

Kate blushed like a youngster at the memory, at the same time experiencing a frisson of anticipation at such a wonderful prospect.

Holding fast to the thought that time heals all things, and feeling, with the tensions resolved between her and Jenny, if not with Danny, that family matters were at last beginning to be easier, Kate felt she could at least allow herself the luxury of daydreaming of a rose-tinted future with Terence. All of which brought her back to the main reason for having chosen Shuggie to do the removal for her despite having to pay him a small tip for his booze money. Big Betty's brother – a dustman – had offered to do the flit with some of his midgie-men pals for nothing other than a cuppa tea and some of Granny's treacle scones, but Kate had declined the kind offer with thanks. The thing was, since Shuggie was her only link with Terence, she wanted the old man to be fully aware of exactly where her new home was situated. Certainly she could just have told him her new address without adopting this all-round-the-houses strategy and have saved herself a bawbee or two at the same time. But this would have meant indicating a need to keep Shuggie informed of her movements … and being the old gossip he was, Shuggie would all too soon have put two and two together. Yes, time enough to tell the world of her interest in and hopes for Terence as and when it actually happened.

Shuggie's voice broke into her thoughts with such abruptness that Kate jumped. "What was that, Shuggie?"

"Ah said, that's the last load now. So Ah'll get back round to the Saltmarket, and Ah'll see you there, Kate."

Kate, Granny, and Hannah settled quickly into their new home and lifestyle and in no time all three were firm favourites with the Irish navvies who lodged there. Granny fussed over and spoiled each and every one of her charges, without now even a mention of her 'poor old rheumaticy back'. Day after day she would stand over the big coal-fired range and bake soda-bread, tattie scones, and pancakes with which to fuel the appetites of a squad of starving navvies. With Hannah, the rough and ready labourers would play endless games of pat-a-cake, I-spy, and even sing jaunty Irish songs to her in whatever precious free time they had at their disposal from the rigours of road-building, bridge construction, canal digging, and the clearing of ditches.

Kate herself, happy both in her work and in her new housing situation, with a fresh bloom on her cheeks, was aware of many an admiring glance from the men in the Hostel. But one, Declan McBanlon, more daring than the rest who had tried to put his arm around Kate and steal a kiss, had very soon got his comeuppance. Still smarting from Kate's icily polite rebuttal of his amorous advances, the brave Declan soon spread the word among his compatriots that … "See that Kate Kinnon. She might be a wizard at the soups and stews … but if you're looking for her to have anything else cooking for you – and I'm bloody sure you all get my meaning – you can just fuckin' forget it. The original ice-maiden, that one."

There was much general hilarity among his mates at this outburst, especially since the bold Declan already had a much-envied reputation as a lady's man and one who had not only kissed the Blarney Stone but who, up till now, had always appeared to have first priority on its magical powers of persuasion.

But for all that, the message of rejection got well and truly across to one and all. The other men at the Hostel, having enjoyed the joke hugely at Declan's expense, now treated Kate with an even greater measure of respect. Kate became increasingly aware of this, she found that in general not only had life become a deal more pleasant, in particular she also had a wonderful back-up team of strong, albeit rough and ready workmen, not one of whom would allow a hair of her head to be touched without her say so.

Even Granny's withered cheeks seemed to have taken on a fresh bloom, so much so, that she almost appeared to blush like a schoolgirl at the merciless yet kind-hearted teasing which was now her daily lot, in dealing with her beloved squad of Irish navvies.

But teasing her or not, to a man they ensured she always had a strong arm on which to lean when descending the stairs to the entrance of the building.

As Granny fussed with wrapping Hannah up warmly for her daily morning stroll and moved with her chair towards the front hall, young Bernard Monaghan called over: "If that's you off jauntin again, Granny, I'm your man. Ah just came off night shift so Ah did, and a wee stroll with my ladyloves 'twill set me off just grand before I crawl into bed."

As the trio went out into the sharp morning air of a clear sunlit December day, Kate leant out to give them a farewell wave. She laughed at the sight of the unshaven, dark-haired pirate of a dashing young man, with a doddery old woman on one arm, pushing Hannah's go chair with his free hand.

Chapter 21

Kate heard her name being almost whispered by a stranger's voice. The soft highland accent, not normally associated with the residents or staff of an Irish Only establishment, immediately sounded alien to her ears.

She turned to face the person who had spoken and saw before her the man-mountain of a 'big Hielan polis', as the Glasgow constabulary were known locally. From the expression on his face, Kate knew instinctively that he had not come on some official business to do with the Hostel. Rather, he was there to give *her* news, news of the very worst kind which related only to her. With a sharp intake of breath, Kate's mind was already flying back down the dark corridors of the years ... back to that far-off day on the Island of Bute when her beloved wee Isabella had drowned in the waters of the so-called Sweet Rothesay Bay.

Kate stared uncomprehendingly at the policeman. His lips were moving, but she heard nothing. Obviously used to dealing with such situations, the constable led Kate over to the nearest chair, sat her down, and brought her a glass of water. Then, when he had her full attention he said: "Mistress Kinnon, from the look of you, I can see that already you've guessed that ... well ... not to put too fine a point on it, it's bad news I'm bringing to your door."

Kate nodded her head and whispered: "It's Granny isn't it? Poor dear old Granny, her heart's given out, hasn't it? Just tell me this ... what hospital has she been taken to? When can I visit her? For she'll be lost without me."

The constable drew over a chair and, sitting directly before Kate, stretched forward, placing a beefy hand on her arm.

"My dear, Mistress Kinnon ... if only it were that simple. It is no hospital in which they rest ..."

Kate put a hand to her mouth in abject terror as the full impact of his words dawned on her.

"They! You said *they*. For God's sake tell me. What has happened? I must know."

The policeman cleared his throat and shifted in his chair.

"It seems the old lady collapsed when crossing the street. The young man was bending over her and let go of the wheel chair the young girl was in. A tramcar came belting round the curve, the horses almost at full gallop – the driver said something had startled them and he couldn't control them. The wheel chair had rolled a bit and the young man either tried to pull it back or to push it clear ... but –"

"No! No, it can't be. Please, dear sweet Jesus ... not that –"

"I'm sorry, my dear. All three. There's just no easy way to say this ... but., all three. The old lady was dead already, I think, and the other two were killed instantly in the collision."

All Irish wakes are memorable, but the one held in the Navvies' Hostel for Granny, Hannah, and Bernard was unique in the annals of Glasgow's Irish community. But with that behind them and the interment having taken place that very afternoon, all Kate now had to get through was the funeral tea itself.

As she busied around the room making sure that every glass was full and each plate had a plentiful supply of tasty bites, she found her thoughts straying back to that other funeral tea almost a year ago ... *Yes, Pearce had certainly had a grand send off and now here, so soon again, I am doing the selfsame service for Hannah and Granny.*

Kate sighed deeply and again went round the room, pausing

here and there to chat with first this one, then that. She was struck yet again by the depth of feeling and compassion all around her.

Father Donovan caught her glance and at once started to make his way over to her.

"Mistress Kinnon. I have already conveyed my condolences to you on your sad loss. Please let me now say how much I appreciate all you have done, and I am bound to say, are still doing here in the Hostel – for the members of my Parish."

Kate flushed and fidgeted with the buttons on her jacket, unsure how, or indeed if, to reply to the compliment from such an unexpected quarter. Never, and she herself would be the first to admit it, but never had she felt comfortable in the company of priests; not even with Pearce's High Anglican priests. However, bearing in mind how true to their own religious beliefs both Granny Gorbals and Bernard had been, Kate took a deep breath, and although even to say the word would probably choke her, Kate realised she could not possibly call the reverend gentleman 'Mister'.

"Father Donovan, thank you kindly for your remarks. And permit me to say how very much your pastoral care meant to both my dear friends."

The priest smiled and nodded acknowledgement of her words before moving on.

Granny and Hannah had both looked so happy that day. That's the picture I'll keep forever in my mind. The pair of them so smartly turned out and with their handsome young escort. Indeed, all a far cry from the days when Granny's old bones were creakingly painful and poor Hannah was screaming out her frustration at the misery of her life.

Kate jumped when a voice at her elbow suddenly seemed to echo her thoughts.

"Aye, Ye had your two girls well turned oot that day, Kate. A real couple of swells. I caught sicht o' them in the street ... and a real bonny sicht they were. It fair gladdened ma auld heart."

As she smiled at Shuggie, Kate felt a sense of déjà-vu for she and the old man had chatted together in much the same comfortable way at Pearce's funeral tea.

"You know Shuggie, we'll have to stop meeting this way ... folk will start talking about us."

Shuggie threw back his head and roared with laughter. This caused a few of the more sober guests to turn and glare. But he was made of sterner stuff and out of sheer devilment he put an arm around Kate's shoulder and whispered in her ear. His words caused her to blush. After a. second's hesitation, she said: "Yes, Shuggie, I do know. But Terence has gone. You don't see him here today, now do you? Last sight I had of him was when he went off on the Irish boat near a month ago. And let's face it, I haven't heard from him since and I don't know when we'll be seeing him again."

Shuggie opened his mouth as if to reply, but then thought the better of it. Before he turned away, however, he gave her a searching look. Then, with a mischievous twinkle in his eye, he said: "You know, my dear old Granny back in Ireland had some wonderful sayings. And any time I was impatient about anything she'd say: 'It won't be long till a wee while.' Kate Kinnon, you can take out of that saying exactly what you want."

And with that cryptic remark he left Kate wondering what precisely their exchange had been all about. The rest of the afternoon passed in a haze and gradually the guests, in varying stages of inebriation, took their leave. When there was just a handful of people left in the room and Kate was wondering how much longer she could keep up her brave front, there was a loud ringing at the front door. Waving aside offers of help, Kate, desperate to keep herself occupied, bustled out into the hallway. But Bridget Scanlon had got there first. As the Hostel's kitchen skivvy threw open the door, Kate gasped as she instantly recognised the tall handsome man who came striding into the hall. His steady, direct gaze focussed on Kate's face and, as their eyes met, it was as if a question had been posed, answered, and settled to their mutual satisfaction.

Terence O'Neil, true to his word, had indeed come back to claim her as his bride. Kate smiled as she thought back to Shuggie's puzzling comment. She realised that the old devil had known full well that this would be yet another reunion on the occasion of a funeral tea. Her life had come full circle.

Now with the promise that, 'It will not be long till a wee while', Kate knew that her life was about to change. Soon, gloriously soon, her new life with Terence would start and no longer would she be the Widow of Candleriggs.

The morning after the funeral tea at the hostel Kate shook her head at the speed with which events had unfolded: the tragic deaths of Hannah, Granny Gorbals, and Bernard; the reappearance of Terence, and his formal proposal of marriage. One minute life seemed settled, if not forever then certainly for some time to come, then seemingly the next minute Kate was arranging to hand over the reins for the Hostel to a young Irish couple virtually straight off the boat at the Broomielaw.

As she stared at her image in the dressing table mirror, Kate sighed. *I was so happy here. It seemed ideal, but now I can't get away quickly enough. I couldn't stay here, I'd see and hear the ghost of Hannah round every corner and eternally feel Granny's presence.*

When she had explained this to Terence after all the funeral tea guests had gone, he had grinned his delight. "Kate, I couldn't be happier. This means that you'll be free of all your responsibilities. Now we can get married right away. Honestly, my dearest love, I must be the happiest man alive."

Kate had coughed nervously. "Not quite right away, Terence. Yes, I do want to marry you but my year-and-a-day won't be up till January twenty-fifth of the new year."

"Damn it, woman, you're enough to make a saint swear. All right. February – the first of February 1902. Where are you going to live until then?"

The young couple who were taking over her duties in the hostel had said she could stay in Granny's old room until she found another place, and Kate hadn't really thought beyond this.

Terence sighed. "You could move in with me –" He held up both hands as if to ward off a blow. "All right! All right. It was just a thought. Why don't you go to Rothesay and spend some time with Jenny and her new husband –"

"Oh, I couldn't do that. I couldn't just move in with them."

"Take a room in one of the boarding houses – there's plenty of them. It will help you and Jenny get properly acquainted again, and let you spoil Theresa –"

"I couldn't afford to live there till February."

"God, Kate. You don't need to worry about that. I can pay. You'll want some time with Jenny before we go back to Ireland –"

"Back to Ireland? For good? What about your business here?"

"Didn't Shuggie tell you? I've given up the book barrow and sold off my other fruit and vegetable barrows."

"Then what will we live on? What will you work at?"

"Did you never wonder why I was off to Ireland so often?"

"Yes, but ... Shuggie once said you bought books over there ... and visited your mother."

Terence laughed. "I visited my mother's lawyer. My mother and I hadn't spoken since my father's funeral years ago. She blamed me for his decline after I ran away from home at eighteen. The sadistic old bastard tried to give me a last thrashing for some imagined fault. He hadn't reckoned that in the time I was away at school I'd grown as tall as him and was just as quick tempered. I had to go back from time to time to sign documents and make sure the lawyer wasn't robbing me blind. That last time I was away was to see to my mother's funeral –"

"Oh Terence, I am sorry."

Terence shrugged. "So am I. I would have liked to make up but my mother was about as obstinate as you. That's why I wanted you and Jenny to put your differences behind you and why I'd like you to meet Danny and his wife. The past is the past and we can't do anything about it, and we don't live forever. Forget and forgive while there's time."

"So do we have a house in Ireland? Can you find a job there?"

"You've seen the house, Kate."

"Oh, that lovely wee cottage Granny and I stayed at during the Fair Fortnight. That would be wonderful, and you can get work from the big house."

Kate looked at Terence in astonishment as he roared with laughter. "What's so funny?"

Finally, wiping his eyes, Terence said: "Kate, Kate. You're certainly no gold digger. Yes, we have the cottage – and the big house. And yes, I will have work from the big house – looking after our affairs."

"You mean –"

"Yes, Kate, you've done it again. You've gone off with the son from the big house, but this time there's no one to cut us off."

Chapter 22

Kate stretched luxuriously and thought: *This is the life. I could do with plenty of this.*

When Terence had suggested she stop at a hotel in Glasgow for a day or so before going to Rothesay to Jenny and Hamish, Kate had resisted the idea. She had never stayed at a hotel in her life, so she could stay on at the hostel for a few days, she had told him. But Terence insisted and here she was with a new wardrobe and a smart leather suitcase neatly stowed in the commodious room at the Central Station Hotel.

A knock on the door startled her. She scrambled out of bed and hurriedly donned the dressing gown Terence had made her buy.

"Yes, who is it?" Kate called through the door.

"Morning tea, ma'am."

Flustered, Kate said: "I didn't order any morning tea."

"No, ma'am, the gentleman who signed you in last night did as he left. There's a note he left on the tray."

On the stroke of nine Kate stood nervously at the entrance to the hotel dining room and looked round for Terence. The maître d' advanced on her and Kate almost fled.

"Good morning, ma'am. Can I help you?"

Before she had time to reply, Terence appeared and took her arm. The maître d' bowed. "If you'll follow me, Mr O'Neil, I have the table ready for you and your fiancée."

"Where did you go last night?" Kate asked. "I thought you were staying here too."

Terence laughed. "What, and have you all worried about gossip with us sleeping under the same roof? I went to my rooms, where I always stay in Glasgow. The rooms you and I could have been sharing this past year if you weren't so damned worried about proprieties and your precious year of mourning."

"Let's not start that again. We've agreed we'll marry in February."

"Have you given any thought to where we'll marry?"

Kate stopped her fork half way to her mouth. *Oh, I hadn't thought of that. Where will we marry? Terence is Catholic and even if I wanted to marry in his church I don't think the priest would let us, with me being Baptist.*

She put her fork down and looked at Terence.

"I thought it would be best if we married in the Registry Office," Terence said. "Save any fuss with priests or ministers, and it's perfectly legal."

"Yes, Pierce and I married in a Registry Office in Belfast. Oh, but what will your priest in Ballygally say?"

"He can say whatever he damned well pleases, but it had better be: 'Good morning, Mrs O'Neil. I hope you are well, Mrs O'Neil,' if he hopes to keep getting the estate's contribution to his parish. I'm what they call a lapsed Catholic. It was another thing I fell out with my mother about. I still go to Mass occasionally – that's how I came to see Danny's wife – and I still give money to the church – some of them, like Father Ryan, actually do some good with the poor when they're not interfering. That's one thing we don't need to worry about. We're not about to have children at our age, so they won't bother us about you not being Catholic and insisting that the children be brought up in the faith."

Kate sighed. "What will your servants think? About me not being Catholic, I mean."

"They can like it of lump it." Terence shrugged. "It's none of their business and work isn't so easy to come by that they'd want to cause any offence to the lady of the house –"

"Oh, the lady of the house! That sounds really grand."

"Besides, Bernadette and Anthony were quite taken with you when you stayed at the cottage in the Glasgow Fair Fortnight. Now, enough nonsense worrying about such things. Let's have some more coffee before we go visiting."

"Visiting? Who are we going to visit?"

"We're going to call on Danny's wife, your daughter-in-law. Don't you scowl at me. She's a nice wee thing and not far short of her time to give you your second grandbairn. If you don't do this now you'll regret it for the rest of your life – Danny's at sea, so you don't need to worry about him and me quarrelling about my being, 'Just a barrow boy and not a suitable acquaintance for a widow of high standing.'"

Kate laughed. "How did you know he'd said that about you?"

"Granny Gorbals told me. She thought it a great joke. The joke will be on Danny when he finds his mother is the lady of the house – a house almost as grand as the Kinnons have."

In the event, Kate was glad she had visited Danny's wife.

Instead of travelling to Govan on the steam tramcar as she had done so often when she worked at Auld Mac's Restaurant, they went in style. Terence whistled up a horse drawn cab from the station and off they went. At Terence's suggestion they left the cab in the street next to Danny's and walked to the close, 'so as not to embarrass the lass with our ostentation.'

Marie was, as Terence had said, a nice wee thing. The single-end was spotless and any surface that could possibly be polished was polished. After the initial reserve on both sides, Kate and Marie chatted like old friends over the obligatory serving of tea and the cutting of the Madeira cake Kate had brought as the traditional Scottish 'wee minding'. Marie laughed heartily at

Kate's telling of amusing incidents in Danny's early life. When they parted it was with promises from Marie to get Danny to write to Kate's new home and to keep Kate informed of the arrival of the baby and its progress.

At the hotel, a note from Jenny, in reply to Kate's asking for the address of a suitable lodging, said that under no circumstances was Kate to stay anywhere but with Jenny and Hamish. Terence, of course, as was only proper, would need to lodge elsewhere.

For the next two days Terence and Kate visited with old friends like Shuggie and Betty, and Kate even had Terence meet Auld Mac and Alec the cook one afternoon after the lunch rush hour had passed.

Finally, they boarded the steamer at Broomielaw to sail for Rothesay – cabin class this time, with Kate shedding a tear as she remembered her last voyage 'doon the watter'.

Part Two

Chapter 1

As Kate sat looking out over sweet Rothesay Bay at the glory of the morning, she could sense the slipping away of the past and all the misery, drudgery, and heartbreak that had gone with it. The glorious God-given scene set out before her not only seemed like a million miles distant in time and space from the bustling ant-hill of Glasgow's Candleriggs, yet at the same time, in some strange way, such natural beauty as this well-named 'Madeira of Scotland' was providing the backdrop for the future ... a future which she and her beloved Terence would share and make their very own.

Still deep in the magic wonderland of her thoughts, Kate jumped in surprise when she heard a voice at her elbow.

"Mother. Honestly, what are you like? I said, and I will say it again ... are you still daydreaming like a lovesick lassie over that Terence O'Neil?"

Kate turned her head, in time to catch the glimmer of amusement in Jenny's eyes. As her own eyes filled, such was the emotion of the moment that Kate could do nothing other than reach out a hand and place it on her daughter's arm. When she could again trust herself to speak, Kate smiled and said: "Jenny, lass, isn't it just truly wonderful how things have turned out? Here you are, happily married to Hamish, in your own wee cottage and a seafront one at that. And here am I, a newly engaged widow-woman, at peace with you, with the world at large and thanking God for all His Blessings. Aye. A strange world altogether."

Jenny wiped away a trickling tear, and for a few moments there was silence between mother and daughter. Then Jenny leant over, gave Kate a great bear hug and finished by whispering words for Kate's ears alone.

As she listened, Kate's eyes widened in surprise.

"Oh, Jenny, my love ... there's no need for you to do all that, to go to so much trouble. Really, my dear, I just don't deserve it. and especially not after all such terrible rows, differences, and emotional battles as you and I have had in the past."

Jenny paused before speaking, as if to draw from some inner reserves of emotion. Then finally she grinned and said: "Listen, Mammy ... what you've just said ... well, is that not exactly why I do want to make such an occasion of your engagement? If nothing else, it will underline the fact that amazingly, and after all these years, we now understand each other so very much better. Not only that, but we are now setting ourselves free, with mutual respect and blessings, to get on with our separate lives, you over in the Emerald Isle of your hopes and dreams and me here in this lovely Island of Bute."

The night of the engagement soiree saw a number of other local weavers and their wives arriving at the seafront cottage at the appointed time. With strong drink soon flowing and the festive table groaning under the weight of what was little short of a banquet, the celebration party, or ceilidh, was soon in full, riotous, glorious swing. Then at exactly the right psychological moment, the door burst open to admit a piper in full Highland regalia. Following close on his heels came Fiona, Jenny's red-cheeked, rotund mother-in-law, bearing aloft a large platter on which in all its mouth-watering glory, posed the most enormous clootie dumplin Kate had ever seen. Shouts of whisky-fuelled delight greeted this Burns Supper-like procession. Then, with the piper weaving his somewhat erratic and obviously inebriated way through the crowd of merrymakers, there was such a marvellous feeling of camaraderie that Kate felt that her heart would burst with happiness.

Once the platter had been safely deposited and given pride of place in the middle of the array of pancakes, shortbread, and treacle scones, Hamish rose to his feet and, to the encouragement of wild cheers from his friends, staggered his way across the room. Once having safely arrived there, he then held on to the edge of the table for some much needed support and thus, more or less securely anchored, he launched into a short but obviously much previously rehearsed speech. But short or not, his best efforts were further truncated by a storm of cheeky catcalls and rude comments from the guests ... not one of whom could have even attempted to wade into the treacherous waters of public speaking and so were now enjoying to the full the spectacle of Hamish dragging himself forever deeper and deeper into such murky and perilous waters.

"Hey, Hamish ... ye might be a helluva good weaver, and, ye're no even aw that bad at coaxin a wee bit tune oota the bagpipes ... but mibbe ye'd better jist leave ony speechifying tae the Meenister when the big day itsel comes aroon. Izzat no right whit Ah'm sayin, Hammie? Eh no?" Was the kindest of the comments.

Loud cheers greeted this comment, followed much good-natured laughter, back slapping, and even miming of Hamish playing his bagpipes. The rumpus quietened momentarily with due and proper respect for the ritual cutting of the clootie dumplin. Then, with each portion ceremonially laid out on plates, the would-be wits yet again got into their stride. On all sides there were giggling remarks and faintly daring but highly suggestive comments addressed to the bride-to-be. These were greeted with unrestrained delight by the knot of people round Kate Kinnon who, by now blushing like an embarrassed schoolgirl, also laughed when the local postie who also held the unofficial post of town gossip called out: "Weel, Mistress Kinnon, let's jist hope that it isnae ye that gets the wee China doll in your slice o dumplin, for fine weel we aw ken whit that would mean ..."

Another voice took up the theme: "Oh aye. Ye could then forget aw aboot dumplins or even wedding cakes ... for it would then hae tae be a christening cake we'd be needin, and pretty damn quick at that. No tae mention mibbe a shotgun forbye, jist tae speed things up a bit, ye ken."

Raucous laughter greeted this gem and once into their stride, there was no holding back the local wags, as immediately there followed yet another drink-induced comment: "No tae forget sumthin else, Jock, whit aboot a new white shawl for the wean ... jist like it says in yon auld sang."

"Aye Man, and that's deid right, Sandy. We must be sure tae hae the bairn lookin aw neat and swanky, like a dumplin in a hanky ..."

The chorus of the well-loved song: "... tae see the baby any time ye care tae call ..." was at once taken up by the revellers. As the strains of their spirited rendition of this jaunty tune died away, into the silence erupted a lone voice.

"Oh aye. That's aw very fine, folks. But jist youse yins, tell me this and tell me nae mair ... if Terence is lucky enough tae get the bachelor button in his dawd o dumplin, whit's tae happen then? Whit Ah want tae ken is this ... whose bum will be hangin oot the windae then, eh? That's the question."

When another outburst of uncontrollable laughter greeted this and seemed in danger of going on forever, Fiona, hands on hips, tried to restore some sort of order. Having spent the entire morning – not to mention a month's supply of raisins and other essential and equally costly household ingredients – in creating the celebration dumpling in the first place, she was not about to see it left lying abandoned on plates and serving no other purpose than being the butt for a raft of rude, ill-considered, and pretty near-the-knuckle jokes.

So with what little dregs of the party spirit she herself could summon up, Fiona assumed an attitude of jocular bonhomie and like an amused yet faintly irritated school-ma'am, she wagged an admonitory finger at the assembled rabble and shouted with all her might above the din: "Weel noo, are youse yins gonnae eat ma clootie dumplin or no? For Ah didnae slave awa in ma kitchen aw day for you lot tae go on a hunger strike and ignore the damn thing, awthegither."

This cry from the heart at least brought a modicum of silence and decorum to the gathering. Thus encouraged, Fiona went on: "So suppose ye jist forget aw aboot bachelor buttons, China baby dolls, and brass wedding rings, there's an important sumthin else that hisnae yet had so much as a mention. Therr's a wheen o silver threepenny bits stowed away inside it as well. So, lads, lassies and even fellow cairters, why don't ye just get stuck into it with a right hearty will. And forbye, guid luck."

A cheer, followed by a stampede towards the well-filled plates, greeted this most welcome announcement.

Alone for almost the first time that evening, suddenly Kate was aware of three things. Firstly she knew that her life was poised to change dramatically; secondly she was fully determined that now having said a mentally envisaged farewell to the Candleriggs, she would not ever again in this life visit that particular district of Glasgow and would even go out of her way to sidestep it when on her way with Terence to board the Irish boat where it lay tied up at the Broomielaw; and finally and perhaps best of all, she now realised that the story, indeed the burden of the saga of the Kinnons of Candleriggs could finally be cast off from her and safely left in the capable and now steady hands of her daughter. From now on, at least as far as Kate was concerned, it would be Jenny's story.

Thus, with all things neatly pigeon-holed and settled in her mind, Kate raised her head to find Terence gazing lovingly at her. Without a word being spoken between them, simultaneously they raised their drinks and joyously clinked the glasses in their unspoken yet fully understood toast. Then, on the point of going to the dining table for a portion of clootie dumplin with a mind to join in the frenetic treasure hunt for the buried threepenny bits, Kate stopped and, laying a hand on Terence's sleeve, said: "Terence, call me a silly, emotional woman if you like, but I would be inclined to say that this is definitely the last great and fond farewell to the Widow of Candleriggs. What do you think?"

Terence's Irish eyes twinkled as he nodded his ready agreement. "All right, Kate ... so, yes, I could not have put it better myself ... yes, you are indeed a silly, emotional woman. But having said that, I do love you with all my heart and soul. And yes, you are absolutely right ... as I usually am ... it is indeed now time, in fact more than high time, to bid farewell to the Widow of Candleriggs."

As their eyes met in the silent communication of a deep and shared love, Kate knew in that moment without a doubt, all was well with her, with her world, and with her very own darling Terence. Then mentally shrugging off the tide of deep emotion which threatened to engulf her and leave her a weeping-with-happiness emotional wreck, she laughed up at her future husband.

"Right. Now we've got that settled and out of the way, why don't we join the treasure hunt?"

Terence gave a great belly laugh, throwing his head back. "Treasure? Treasure, did you say, Kate? Somehow I don't really think the odd threepenny bit rescued from the innards of a clootie dumpling is going to feature all that large in our lives, do you, Kate?"

Kate laughed, knowing as she did exactly what area of their future life together Terence was referring to but without spelling it out for her at that moment.

Then arm-in-arm and as if sharing a wonderful secret which they alone knew, they headed towards the table, their guests, and whatever Fate had in store for them in their future life together.

The wonderful evening ended as it had begun, with goodwill on all sides, much eating and even more drinking. Towards the end, for those matrons who could never envisage going out into the cold night air of the west coast of Scotland without it, there was the ritual cup of tea, and the party broke up.

Terence kissed his fiancée a fond goodnight before he set out along the seafront in search of his lodgings at Mrs Walker's wee boarding establishment situated just beyond the Skeoch Woods.

Having had all her offers of clearing up in the kitchen firmly repulsed by Jenny, Kate headed for bed, knowing that although tired, she would be too excited to sleep. In any case, she was already living the dream. And who could ask, far less dare to hope for anything more in this life? Yes, life had now turned full circle for Kate Kinnon and, as she said her bedtime prayers on her knees, she thanked God and His angels for all their blessings.

Chapter 2

It was the morning after the hugely successful engagement party and a housewifely Jenny bustled to and from the kitchen and the best room, clearing up the detritus left in the aftermath of the ceilidh. From time to time she would burst into snatches of song. Not that she ever had been much of a singer – and Jenny would be the first to admit this – but the spontaneity, happiness, and sheer joie de vivre springing from her entire being leant a certain indefinable charm to the old Scottish songs she was favouring. She was just launching into a spirited rendition of Charlie is My Darlin', when hearing a sound behind her, she turned around in time to see Hamish, with hands on hips and a mock furious expression on his face.

"Oh ho! So what's this, Jenny? If Charlie is yer darling, jist what does that make me? Now hold on a minute. Don't tell me … just let me guess. Ah've got it. Ah'm supposed tae be yer fancy man, that's it, isn't it?"

Jenny's sudden intake of breath was proof enough of her shocked sensibilities, without what she then went on to say: "A fancy man, Hamish. What a terrible thing to say to me, your own legally married wife. A fancy man, indeed, how can ye even joke about such a thing, especially after how honest I was with you before we married about all that sort of thing and my horrendous past and …"

A firm believer in the concept that actions always spoke louder than words, Hamish caught hold of her shoulders, turned his wife around to face him and ended by taking her in his arms. He then silenced her as yet still chattering mouth with a long, lingering, satisfying kiss. They were still in this embrace when Kate came into the room. Catching sight of the engrossed and happy pair, Kate laughed softly, turned on her heel, and was on the point of returning to the best room when, flushed and eyes sparkling, Jenny broke free of her husband's arms.

"Mammy! Aren't you the one that's early this day, and it must be said, bright-eyed and bushy tailed into the bargain. Honestly dear, I thought you would be having a wee rest, a well deserved one at that, especially after all the excitement of the party last night. Not to mention the fact that it was well into the wee small hours before you finally got to your bed."

Well aware that Jenny was babbling on in an effort to hide her embarrassment, Kate nodded quickly in the hope of stemming the onrush of words. So without giving her daughter the slightest chance to launch yet again into yet another river of rhetoric, Kate said: "Well, you're quite right of course, and now that you come to mention it, I did think of long lie. But when wee Theresa popped in beside me for an early morning cuddle ... well ... any luxurious thoughts of even attempting to lie in late, all such selfish nonsense just went flying out of the window."

Jenny, now smoothing down the nest of her hair, opened her mouth to reply, but her mother had not yet finished speaking.

"No, I simply kissed goodbye to any idea of allowing myself the unheard of luxury of any long lie. In any case, and, as you well know from your childhood days, I have always been an early riser. All to do with habit and sheer necessity, I suppose. Anyway, I'm pretty sure by now Terence will be setting out from his lodgings. So, I thought I would take a wee bit of a stroll along the seafront and hopefully meet up with him at the halfway mark. So, 'bye now, folks. I'm really sorry to have disturbed your lovely romantic interlude. But I'll leave you now to your own devices. See you soon, 'bye."

With these words and a cheery wave of her gloved hand, Kate left the cottage. As they heard the front door close behind her, Jenny and Hamish, like two youngsters caught in some misdemeanour, looked shamefacedly at each other. Then as Jenny started giggling, her husband, scratching his head in bemused bewilderment, said in his soft Scottish voice: "Well, Jenny ... that really must be true love! Can't say that I would ever see ye braving the driving rain on a morning like this to go out of yer way to come and meet me."

Jenny, with gales of laughter, lifted a wooden spurtle from the porridge pot aloft as her makeshift weapon, pretending to launch an attack on her husband. The door once again opened, this time to admit Theresa. Seeing such a skirmish being played out before her very own eyes, the toddler's lower lip started to tremble, then as her eyes filled with ready tears, she started to cry. It was all left to Hamish who immediately swept up in his arms his already much adored and hopefully soon to be legally adopted young daughter. "There, there, ma wee darling, dinnae upset yersel like this, ma lovely wee chookie hen." He held her trembling body close and stroked her long silken hair, at the same time making eye contact with Jenny over the top of Theresa's head. Although not another word was spoken between husband and wife, both knew a message had been given and received. As unobtrusively as she possibly could, Jenny put the wooden spoon back into its former resting place inside the blacklead porridge pot. That safely done, she then waited with what patience she could muster for the moment when Theresa, sufficiently comforted and calmed down, might be handed over to her.

At last, with a still quietly sobbing Theresa cuddling in close to her, Jenny tried to explain as best she could in the simplest language that: "Mummy and Daddy were just pretending to have a fight, my wee darling. That was all. It was just a silly joke ... And do you know something, else, sweetheart, it really wasn't even all that funny after all, now was it, my pet?"

While Theresa gave a faint nod of agreement with this theory, it was soon clear it would take rather more than just a few such pacifying weasel words to restore her to her normal sunny humour. It was abundantly clear that some sort of enticing inducement would be required before the now 'tear-begrutten' toddler would be willing to forego in any way her stance of hard-done-by and thoroughly disgruntled offspring. When a biscuit and even a finger of shortbread had been forcefully rejected and flung with wildest abandon to the furthest corner of the kitchen by a whimpering Theresa, the next offering fared but marginally better. At least this time, it did manage to produce the ghost of a smile, albeit a rather watery and pale imitation of her usual cheery grin. The fistful of vanilla tablet which had been thrust into her hand together with the somewhat rash promise that Hamish would later take the chubby toddler for a piggieback ride through the nearby Skeoch Woods, finally dried up the last of her tears. Added to that was the icing on the cake, so to speak, when Jenny, "cross my heart and hope to die," gave the promise to her daughter that she could have her very own farewell party for Granny Kate and Terence.

Even more than that; she would be allowed to help Mummy with the baking. With the wonderful mental picture of, once apron-donned, getting to scrape out the cake mixture bowls and eat the remnants, Theresa finally toddled off quite happily. Again left to their own resources, Hamish gave his wife a quizzical look.

"Ye know something, dear? Ye would hae made a marvellous teacher. Listening to ye and yer diplomatic way of dealing with wee Theresa, Ah could almost picture ye in a classroom with all yer pupils hanging on yer every word. Aye, Ah kin see it aw in ma mind's eye."

Instead of the ready laugh or even the peck on the cheek which he had confidently expected as his reward for heaping on her head such a fine compliment, Hamish, to his amazement, saw his wife back away from him. Then her face darkened and her lovely eyes clouded over, as though at some distant yet vividly remembered emotional turmoil, some deep trauma which she had obviously thought had been deeply buried, never again to be brought out into the light of day. As Hamish put out a hand towards her in a vain attempt to offer some little comfort, his wife waved away any such tender loving care, together with the words, words which seemed dredged up from her very soul: "Leave it, Hamish. Do not even ask, I beg of you. Just, for God's sake, leave it. And don't ever, ever again make any such reference as to my being such a thing as a born teacher. Got that?"

Still completely in the dark as to what he had done or was supposed to have said, Hamish, in an attempt to lighten the weird situation, grinned sheepishly and said: "Anyway, leaving that flea sticking to the wall, as the old saying goes, there is one other matter. Correct me if Ah'm wrong, but somehow back there, before Ah so obviously put my foot in it in one way or another, Ah rather got the impression ye actually said to Theresa something about another party?"

Jenny made no effort to reply, so it was left to Hamish to continue: "Another party? Did Ah hear aright? And if Ah am correct, did ye really mean that or was it just idle words to pacify the bairn?"

Jenny nodded, then with head cocked, the expression on her face making it clear that she still had not forgiven him, she said: "Oh, that's charming, I must say! Absolutely charming! So now you think that I am in the business of making empty promises. No, Hamish, you did not imagine any such promise. You did hear aright ... indeed I did ... I do mean exactly what I said. We will have another party. But having said that, mind you, before you get too excited there's one thing I should point out to you. This time it will be strictly teetotal, with no strong drink of any kind, and for immediate family only."

As Hamish digested this piece of information, his wife her good humour partially restored, smiled gently at him and said: "One other point ... wee Theresa can help me bake some special fairy cakes. We Kinnons, Glesga keelies or not, we do have our own traditional family recipe for them, you know. So it's maybe time I was starting to train Theresa in the making of them, young enough as she is."

Hamish laughed, not only in relief that whatever it was he had said to so irk his wife was now safely behind them, but also at the mental picture of Theresa as a young baker. That apart and keen as he was to maintain the peace between them, he smiled his agreement with what Jenny now chose to do. Placing a hand on her arm he said: "All right, ma wee darlin'. Whatever pleases ye will be just fine with me. Mind ye, Ah still cannae see what's so very special about your common or garden fairy cakes. But if there's tae be nae strong intoxicating liquors, there is just one thing …"

As willing to please her husband as he so obviously was to please her in trying to make amends for his damning comment on the subject of teachers, Jenny again smiled and nodded for her husband to go on.

"If as ye say, there's tae be nae booze … can ye please jist make sure that Theresa, the baker, makes plenty of them wee cakes, so that there's enough to go round. Otherwise, we'll end up with what folks long ago used to call a tea-n-toast struggle. Ah mean, the watter of life is one thing, but we cannae hae guid folk goin' hungry forbye, noo can we?"

Jenny smiled, by now thoroughly intrigued. "I didn't knew you were so knowledgeable, Hamish. A tea-n-toast struggle, indeed. I can't say I've ever heard that expression before."

Hamish grinned. "A man of hidden talents, that's me. Come to think of it, I suppose that's where the saying 'bun fight' comes from too. And while we're at it, one more gem of knowledge for ye, Jenny … The poor spinsters of the Parish who used to attend such frugal soirees … they were aye cried tea-kettle purgers. Now what dae ye think o that, eh? Mind you, I suppose yon poor hungry souls would have been fair glad of even a wee tasting of Theresa's fairy cakes."

"Now then, Hamish, don't you dare to go making fun of the special Kinnon cakes. You see, Mammy always used to make them as a particular treat for Hannah, God rest, her soul, and ... well ... when you think about it, it's one of our long held family traditions that brings back memories. So let me just say, it will mean a lot to Mammy, especially if she later learns that her darling wee Theresa's podgy sticky fingers have had a part in their baking."

There was nothing else to be said at this point so, always true to his policy of actions speaking louder than words, Hamish drew his wife toward him and planted a lingering kiss on her cheek. With a cheery wave he turned to leave and muttered jokingly to himself: "They'll be calling me a tea-kettle purger next when my workmates get wind of Theresa's party."

Then louder so that Jenny would hear him, his parting shot was: "Uch Ah've been cried worse than that in my time. And even if health and wealth have missed me," he misquoted from the famous poem, Ah can aye say with heart and voice ... Jenny kissed me."

Chapter 3

The ensuing weeks passed all too quickly and with even Theresa's farewell party for Granny Kate and Terence now being but a memory, it was clear that the departure of the happy couple could be put off no longer. Both Jenny and Hamish had tried to delay the inevitable goodbyes. With his wife's prompting, Hamish had even suggested that they forget Ireland and instead make the Island of Bute the venue for their wedding ceremony and its attendant celebrations. While it was indeed a tempting prospect, both couples knew that such change of plans at this stage would simply be a case of postponing the already dreaded day of departure, with its resultant separation. Finally, it was left to Terence to spell out what was little short of an ultimatum. The words he chose left both Jenny and Hamish looking at each other in amazement. Terence's announcement had been greeted by a stunned silence which was broken only when a frowning Hamish said: "Look Terence, all right, we do know that we've kept ye and Kate here quite long enough. We fully understand that ye want to get back over to Ireland for yer planned wedding. But what was it ye said about yer staff getting anxious? Please don't think I'm being rude, but one thing does occur to me. Surely a barrow boy like ye doesnae run to the expense of employing a housekeeper and other staff for a wee cottage or a but-and-ben."

Terence and Kate exchanged a conspiratorial glance. As if gathering his thoughts, Terence again looked at Kate, as if seeking help or affirmation of what he knew he must now reveal.

At a faint nod from her, Terence took a deep breath. "Hamish, Jenny, there's something you need to know. But perhaps you had better sit down for this."

Sensing that some sort of family conference might be in the making, Jenny – ever now the gracious hostess – at once said: "Well, if your news is to be so shocking that we have to sit down to hear it, perhaps a cup of tea might help things along? After all let's face it, it isn't every day that I hear my poor Mammy is about to be swept off to the wilds of Ireland."

"No, Jenny," Terence said. "Just sit down and listen. Yes, I was a barrow boy. I had six other barrows apart from the book barrow. When I fell out with my parents and came to Scotland I had some cash – not much – and I found when I worked with one of the fruit barrows that if you knew what you were doing you could make quite a tidy profit buying for yourself at the market and selling at a fair mark-up from your barrow. The old man I was working with was quite willing to let me buy him out with the little cash I had come with. Within five years I had six barrows with men running them for me. I still did all the buying at the market every day. Browsing at one of the book barrows I learned that there was a good profit to be made buying and reselling university text books. I was always more interested in books than I was in fruit and vegetables. So I invested in a book barrow and decided to run it myself, buying books by the yard at estate sales and auctions, and from university students wanting to cash in on books they no longer needed."

"Fine," Hamish said, "so ye made a good living from your barrow business. Enough to buy yersel a place in Ireland? Is that the staff ye're worried about? You've got a wheen o' barrows over there and lads tae run them – staff ye call them?"

"Now, Hamish, don't be rude. Terence is a businessman; of course he would be worried about the running of his business."

Terence laughed. "I'm sorry. I shouldn't have got started on my barrows. I came to Scotland to get away from my father. He and I had fallen out – it doesn't really matter now what about. He was a gentleman farmer. Nothing all that grand –"

Hamish snorted. "Oh, aye, we've got some o' them on Bute tae. Live aff other folk's hard work –"

"Hamish, that's enough," Jenny said. "Terence is a guest in this house."

"It's all right, Jenny," Terence said. "Strangely enough what Hamish said sounds very like what I quarrelled with my father about. Didn't someone once say or write, 'All men are revolutionaries in their youth but conservatives when they are older'? Anyway, we have four farms we rent out and a home farm. I showed I could live by my own efforts and put aside a few shillings in my years in Glasgow, enough to live on for quite a while, so I'm not ashamed to go back and claim what's mine. We won't be wealthy, but we'll be very comfortable."

There was a tense, silence then Hamish said: "We're glad for you and Kate, I'm sure, but we'll not be taking any charity from you –"

"Good." Terence smiled. "None was being offered. Now, Jenny, you said something about tea?"

Chapter 4

The twins, Glen and Gordon, were the most adorable babies that had ever graced this earth. Certainly that was the opinion of their parents, their Rothesay grandparents, neighbours, friends, and their three-and-a-half year-old step-sister Theresa when they were born in June of 1902. The latter soon abandoned her rag doll Hazel in favour of the two real live dollies with their podgy little fingers and toes. And every time that Granny Fiona and her husband Wattie came into the cottage, there would the usual oohing and aahing and yet again loud cries of: "Isn't it wonderful that the wee boys will grow up to be true Brandanes!"

At first Jenny was not too sure what this oft acclaimed accolade meant but a whispered consultation with Hamish soon enlightened her. People who had actually been born on the Island of Bute were entitled to call themselves Brandanes and this was counted a very real and honourable distinction with which to set out on life. It was not uncommon to hear people inject extraneously into even the most mundane conversation the magic phrase of: "Of course, I'm a Brandane."

So here now living in Bramble Cottage were these two bonnie babies, Brandanes to their fingertips. If Jenny and Hamish were proud parents, then their own joy was as nothing compared to the euphoria of Fiona and Wattie. Their Brandane grandparents positively doted on Glen and Gordon.

There was one person in the Darroch household, however, whose enthusiasm for the twins seemed to diminish somewhat as the boys grew from charming babies to rumbustious toddlers – the terrible twos. It was thanks to the fact of Hamish pointing it out to her that Jenny first became aware that there might just be something of a problem evolving. But when it was actually spelt out to her, and at regular intervals at that, even then Jenny still found it hard to accept.

"Hamish, you're talking nonsense. Why on earth would Theresa be in any way jealous? Honestly, man, I just cannot think what you're on about."

Hamish simply raised a quizzical eyebrow. "Lassie, lassie. Think aboot it. For all her life until now, she was the adored only child. And ye ken yourself, Granny Kate doted on her. But poor wee Theresa nowadays, short of setting sail over the Irish sea, she cannae even go running to her Granny Kate's arms for wee bit of comfort and a grandmotherly cuddle."

Jenny frowned and was about to speak but Hamish went on: "Ah mean tae say, ma ain mither, gie her her due, she aye does her best to include Theresa in everything, but let's face it, we might as well be honest, she just cannae see beyond her ain favourites, her very ain wee Brandane twins. Fine well ye ken how she's aye gloatin' aboot that. Ah'm damn sure ye don't need me tae remind ye on that particular score, is that no richt, Jenny?"

Jenny pursed her lips, all too aware that this constant boast, like some latter day Greek chorus, was most certainly wearing a bit thin. This was this especially the case since she felt instinctively it was sometimes directed, albeit in a roundabout way, at herself, the only Glaswegian in their midst. In the early days of the marriage ... and with its being common knowledge that Hamish had jilted a Brandane girl when he had fallen head over-heels in love with Jenny ... there had been a certain 'coolth' between Fiona and her 'Glesga Keelie' daughter-in-law. At least the birth of the twins some ten months after their wedding had helped establish an uneasy alliance of sorts between the two women and had brought Jenny into the family fold rather more than would otherwise have been possible. But even at that, with their unarmed truce, it was clear that the two women would never be in any really comfortable relationship together.

Still deep in thought, Jenny jumped when she heard Hamish's voice from the doorway. "Well, Jenny, Ah've said ma piece, and Ah'll try no tae harp on aboot the matter any mair. Ye've harkened weel tae ma words, and ye can believe them or no as ye like. But one thing Ah will say yet again ... for God's sake, please at least keep an eye on Theresa when she's anywhere near tae the twins. Just remember, ma dear lassie, an jist don't ye ever forget these words ... jealousy is a powerful emotion. It can be, and all too often is, a powerful, destructive force in anyone's life. Jist you mark my words. Don't think ye can come runnin' tae me when it strikes its evil onslaught in this hoose. Ah've said my bit, and as far as Ah'm concerned, that's the end of the matter. The rest is up tae ye ... after all ye're her mother. She's yer bairn and yer responsibility."

Although severely shaken by what her husband had said, Jenny had mentally dismissed his dire warnings of any possible harm her first-born could or would ever inflict on the adored twins. Even so, and ever aware that she herself – if she were being strictly honest – now favoured the boys over an increasingly dour, miserable, and withdrawn Theresa, she still conveniently ignored warning signs of approaching disaster. She chose to accept her husband's ultimatum that no further discussion on the subject could be entered into. But having agreed to such a wall of silence on that particular subject, the unspoken words and anxieties had most decidedly become something of an issue between them and for the first time in their three years of idyllic marriage, suddenly all was not well in the Darroch household. Matters finally came to a head one Friday dinnertime when, arriving home for his one o'clock meal, Hamish came into a room in which all hell had seemingly broken loose. Gordon and Glen were screaming their little heads off as Theresa, with a demonic leer of utter delight and satisfaction, was jabbing the end of a steel knitting needle into their bare legs.

Hamish took in the situation at a glance. Then, although not a man normally given to displays of ill temper, a now purple-faced Hamish yanked the knitting needle from his step daughter's hand and threw the offending weapon into the furthest corner of the room. That done, and with his fury now focused on the assailant herself, he was within an inch of giving the jealous little bitch the thrashing of her young life, when the door opened to admit a frowning Jenny, obviously come to investigate the rumpus. With his hand raised in anger and a cowering Theresa now clutching a chair for some much needed support, Hamish stopped in mid action, like some stone carved statue in which only the eyes could move, and stared at his wife.

"Jenny, I've warned ye to look out for something like this. But no, ye wouldn't hear a word of it, not a single whisper would ye listen to against yer darling daughter. She's gone too far this time. Would ye just look at the boys' wee legs, pouring with blood so they are; that's the work of yer precious daughter."

With a questioning look at Theresa, Jenny went across to examine the twins, sure that Hamish had grossly exaggerated whatever it was that had supposedly happened. But one look at the twins and Jenny took in the situation at a glance. At a loss as to how best to cope with such an explosive state of affairs, Jenny instinctively went on the defensive as she shouted back at her husband.

"Oh, so suddenly she's just *my* daughter? I know you have hinted at such these past few weeks but then we seemed to have something of a truce. But two weeks back you were supposed to be adopting her. Now just tell me that's not true."

Hamish lowered his hand. Theresa, taking advantage of the lull in proceedings, and under cover of her mother and stepfather's shouting the odds at each other, got to her feet and, with all possible speed, ran out of the room.

Approaching his wife with a wild look in his eyes, Hamish

said: "Jenny, you know as well as I do, I'm never much good at all that business with legal documents, and anyway, lawyers cost a hell of a lot of money. But as you know, the intention was there and ... But dammit it all, woman, if you think I'm about to go down that memory lane at a time like this, forget it. Anyway, listen to me, woman, and listen good ... ye can sort out today's mess, for one thing's sure, it's yer brat that's created this torment, and unless she's stopped right now, will go on causing such havoc. And I for one will not have it. Do you hear? And while ye're at it ye can forget about feeding me any dinner this day. I feel sick to my stomach. This matter must be addressed now. So, ye can just find that daughter of yers and gie her the worst skelpit bum of her life."

Jenny, by now shaking with anger and almost incandescent with rage, shouted back: "Oh, so the master of the house has spoken has he?"

Hamish took a step nearer, raised a hand, a bunched fist, as if about to strike a blow on her upturned face. Then, as if awakening from a nightmare, he stopped, turned his head and gazed in disbelief at his own upturned and now trembling hand.

Finally, with a face as if carved from stone, he again stared at his wife for what seemed an endless time. Then his shoulders slumped, he looked down at his feet; suddenly in that instant, a broken, defeated man, he shuffled from the room. Even had he banged the front door behind him, it might have showed there was some spirit left in him, it might have proved he would still have the gumption to return to the fight later on. But the biting wind now rushing through from the open front door was proof enough of the fact ... Hamish had not even had the will, far less the energy to close the door of the cottage to protect his wee family from the cruel winds then roaring in from the seafront.

Somehow, for Jenny, in some strange symbolic way his failure either to close the door gently, or even to bang it in frustration, underlined the situation and spoke of two things. Quite apart from it being a situation which need never have happened, two matters stood out like sentinels in their life ... a chapter of their formerly happy marriage had come to its conclusion and Hamish, her own darling husband Hamish, had lost the will to fight, he had conceded defeat. Then, as sobbing wracked her body, Jenny was left with the feeling – indeed the utter conviction – she herself was to blame and nothing in Bramble Cottage would ever be the same again. She gathered the twins to her bosom and, nestling into the soft, sweet smelling, rosy-appled cheeks, she moaned: "What have I done? Dear God almighty, what have I done letting poor Hamish go off like that, without even a crust of bread and a bowl of soup to fill his belly? How will the poor soul be able to do his work at the mill? He'll be starving, not having broken bread since his porridge."

But even as she forced her mind to concentrate on such mundane matters as food or the lack of it, Jenny knew in her heart of hearts what was the real issue of that morning's chaos and confrontation. Above all, she knew it would not be easily resolved. The bottom line was it was all her own stupid fault for not having listened to Hamish in the first place.

Chapter 5

In the normal way, Hamish would arrive back from his day's work at the mill somewhere round six-thirty. However, as Jenny herself well knew, today had been anything but normal, so she was not too surprised when the hour of seven came and went; still there was no sign of her husband. But as the hands on the wag-at-the-wall crept ever nearer to eight o'clock, at first she began to worry, then later her concern turned to anger as she thought: *Damn the man. I know he's probably just trying to teach me a lesson, but apart from that, surely he can admit to himself he's bound to be starving by now, so this really is beyond a joke, if in fact it ever was a joke in the first place. Surely to heavens he must realise I'll have made him a special meal to make up for our row this morning. And angry or not, surely he'll have felt the pains, the gnawing pains of an empty belly, having missed out on his usual mid-day meal.*

With the three children packed off early, settled down for the night, there was silence, a blessed peace in the cottage, all the more appreciated after the chaos of the morning's rowdy scenes. From time to time, Jenny went to the window and peered out into the cold wet night, as if in this way, she could somehow speed the arrival of her husband. But crane her neck all she liked and strain her eyes into the murky darkness, still there was neither sign nor sound of Hamish. By now thoroughly ashamed of her behaviour earlier in the day, all Jenny wanted was for Hamish to arrive home safely, late or not, so that she might greet him with a wifely kiss and at once deliver to him the apology which she had been mentally rehearsing for the past few hours. A last look out of the window, then with a sigh of resignation she settled down as best she could beside the oil lamp and took up a pile of darning. She was still engaged in this most hated of domestic chores when, thinking she had heard a sound, she threw down the bundle of socks from her lap and rushed round to the door. But whether it had been her imagination or the deer come down from the hills behind the house, she would never know. Anyway, there was nothing to be seen and, of Hamish, still not a sight. Resuming her attack on the socks, she found that what little concentration she had had previously was now gone completely as all the while raced through her mind the thought: *Where on earth can he be? Perhaps he's gone out in a great sulk to his beloved mother's house out at Port Bannatyne?*

But much as she would have liked to have drawn a measure of comfort from such a ready made solution to the puzzle, she knew in her heart of hearts this was most definitely not the answer. While quite clearly, as had been indicated to her in so many ways over the years, she was definitely not Fiona's first choice of a suitable wife for her wonderful son, the strict Bible-carrying church-goer believed implicitly in the sanctity of marriage. That being the case, the strict moral code to which mother-in-law Fiona firmly adhered, would clearly have no truck in even attempting to shield her son, beloved or not, from the wrath of his legally wed wife. Marital rows and wifely upsets were common enough in any family but even so they were always best left strictly confined to the two people most intimately concerned ... and that did not include any interfering busybody of a mother-in-law, no matter how well intentioned her motives might be. Following this train of thought, Jenny had to admit Fiona had indeed always tried to be impartial and certainly, since the birth of the twins, her once hated mother-in-law had mellowed somewhat in her attitude.

Jenny was still deep in thought when a sudden knocking at the door roused her into action. When she opened the door it was to find Duncan Ross, another weaver, on her doorstep. The man was twisting his tweed bunnet in his hands and was clearly in an agony of indecision as to what he was about to say to his workmate's wife. Jenny beckoned for him to enter the cottage, all the while wondering what on earth she was about to hear. Despite his obvious discomfort, he behaved as if he were the master of the house and she the guest when with a wave of his hand, he said: "Ah think mibbe ye'd better sit doon, Mistress Darroch." Immediately, at the implication of something being dreadfully wrong, Jenny gasped and put an already trembling hand to her mouth. In a strangled voice which she barely recognised as her own, she said: "Duncan, what is it? Something has happened, hasn't it? For God's sake tell me. What terrible news have you brought to my door?"

The weaver nodded, scarcely able to mask his own upset at whatever it was that had befallen his work companion. Again he nodded, gave a nervous cough and finally came out with: "Aye, it's Hamish. It's like this, there's nae easy way for me to say this … so Ah'd better jist spit it oot and be done with it. There's been an accident, a terrible accident doon at the mill."

Jenny felt the colour drain from her face as Duncan went on: "Weel, Hamish agreed for to dae an extra shift, a late shift like. He said he was in nae great hurry tae get hame. Weel, he was working awa … That's when it happened … and the awful thing is … if he'd stopped his work … quit at the usual time, there would hae been nae problem whatsoever. God help him, he should never have offered tae dae that extra shift. Ah ken him weel and I could see he wisnae quite hissell … seemed awfie tired and a bit oota sorts, if ye get my meaning. He even complained tae me at one point aboot feeling a bit wabbit with pangs of hunger. Oh God, if only he had stopped work at his usual time and came hame as normal tae his wife and his wee bairns and …"

Jenny, by now like one possessed, grabbed hold of Duncan's hand and screamed at him: "For God's sake, Duncan, will you just stop going all round the house with your story. Just tell me exactly what has happened to my poor man. I must know."

Still standing by the kitchen table, Duncan clutched it for support. There was a second's silence as he continued to stare at her. Then the words poured from him.

"Hamish, like Ah said, couldnae hae been gienin the work his full attention. Onywie, he got his arm caught up in the machinery and … well, the Doctor had to cut him free. The only way tae dae that … was … he had to amputate. He's still alive, but Ah maun say, if Ah'm being honest, he's only just alive and nae mair and noo he's lying unconscious in the hospital."

How Jenny got through the rest of that horrendous night she would never know. One thing she did know, her good man was now an amputee, but which arm she still had to find out.

Chapter 6

When Hamish had first came home from the hospital, he was depressed, irritable, and dour, but above all, he was angry. No matter what his wife did, said, or even attempted to do or say, it was never enough. Each time she tried, with the best will in the world, to fuss over him, the end result was the same. With his remaining arm, he would shake her off and shout: "Get away from me, woman. For God's sake, leave me alone. It's thanks to ye Ah'm now a cripple and no amount of fussing over me is ever going to change that. But if ye've conveniently forgotten already just how this bloody disaster came about, just let me remind ye. The only reason Ah worked late on that hellish night was this ... Ah just couldnae bear to come home to ye any earlier. There now, woman, has it finally sunk into your stupid brain?"

With such ill feeling almost a physical presence in the cottage, this atmosphere affected the behaviour of the three children. Not a day went past but what it was filled with shouting, weeping, temper tantrums, and ongoing rows about nothing and everything. Not that this was all Jenny had to worry about. With no money now coming into the household, she was at her wits' end in constantly trying to scrape together enough oats, barley, potatoes, and flour with which to feed her family. Thanks to the help of Fiona and Wattie, and having used up their meagre life savings, this month's rent and the rent for some months ahead had been duly paid. But even so, in the dark reaches of the night, Jenny constantly worried about the future. What in God's name was to become of them all? And what had been her dream-come-true, their idyllic life in Bramble Cottage ... was all that really now going to end in tears, acrimony and disaster?

One morning as Hamish sat bowed over a mug of weak tea, suddenly he looked up and said: "Things cannae go on like this for much longer, woman. Something will have to be done. There's really only one thing for it now."

When Jenny greeted this remark in stony silence, Hamish frowned at her. "God Almighty, have ye gone deaf as weel as daft? Jenny, Ah've said it once, but Ah'll say it again ... there's only one thing left to do now. And if ye weren't so blind ye'd have realised it already for yersel. One thing left to us, to this dig us out of this pit of poverty and misery ..."

His wife raised her head. She pushed back a lock of stray hair as if in this way, clearing her forehead of all encumbrance, she would then see more clearly what it was her apology for a husband was now going on about.

"One avenue left to us, is that what you're saying? All right, so let's hear your brilliant suggestion, for God alone knows, we could do with all the help that might be available to us, from whatever quarter. But one thing you should perhaps bear in mind, there would be no point in asking your parents for help. We've already, bled them dry. So, what is this magical solution you now seem to have conjured up? Spit it out, Hamish."

"Jenny, ye've just said it yersel ... from whatever quarter the help might come ... Surely ye realise what Ah'm talking about? Or dae Ah hae to spell it all out for ye?"

By now Jenny was pretty sure in what particular direction his thoughts were heading, but obstinate to the last, she determined to keep silent in order to make Hamish be the one to put the proposed plan into words.

At length when it dawned on him that Jenny had no intention of making it any easier for him, Hamish said: "Ah'm talking about Kate, of course. Let's face it, we all know yer dear mother has really come up in the world since she married into money. She's forever going on in her letters about her big house, isn't she? Every letter she sends ye, it's her big house this, and her servants that ... but she never thinks to send ye any money, now does she?"

Jenny flushed but this time rose to the bait. "Hamish, just you leave my mother out of this. You yourself said before they left that you wouldn't accept charity from Terence. In any case, she doesn't know just how bad your accident was. I've been a wee bit economical with the truth each time I write to her. After the hard life she had over all those years in the Candleriggs the last thing I want to do is to cause her any more grief or worry."

Hamish's face flushed red. "Oh that's marvellous, bloody marvellous, Ah must say. It's all fine and dandy to worry my parents out of their heads with agonising over our plight and allow them to spend their hard-won meagre savings on us. But it would never do to upset the grand lady Kate, now would it?"

"Hamish, you can forget the sarcasm, if you don't mind. I'll not be asking Kate for help of any kind, and that's final. If our situation is all that desperate, you are right in that there's now only one thing left to do ... you can get up off your backside and be man enough to go out and get a job."

By now fit to be tied, her husband gave a snort of disgust. "A job? Me? Get a job? Have you lost all reason, woman? Who in their right mind is ever now going to pay for my daily darg, me, a one-armed, left handed weaver. Just-answer me that, woman!"

Again that terrible silence between them, as they sat with their bitter thoughts. Then Jenny's face cleared and in a voice loud with positive optimism, she said: "Right, that's it then. If you can't or won't get work, just you stay at home, wallow in misery and self-pity and when you have a spare moment, look after the bairns. If you can't work at the mill, then I sure as hell can. Believe me, with my years of experience at Templeton's Carpet Manufactory in Glasgow, they'd soon enough take me on. All that valuable experience must count for something."

If Jenny had set out deliberately to hurt and wound her husband she could not have done a better job. As if he had been struck a physical blow, Hamish backed away from her in horror. Even before he actually spoke, the stricken look on his face said it all for him.

"Ah don't believe this. Ye, a woman and supposedly a loyal wife ... ye would actually, in cold blood, strip away like that whatever dignity of my manhood Ah hae left? Ye would abandon me, me the head of the household and the master in my own cottage, me left to the mopping up of children's vomit and the wiping of their bums. All that, while ye are seen by all and sundry as the breadwinner, the sainted martyr and the saviour of our benighted family."

Jenny opened her mouth to protest at his interpretation of her selfless offer, but her husband had not yet finished his tirade. He banged a bunched fist down on the deal table, causing an enamel plate to clatter to the floor. "No wife of mine will ever set foot in that or in any other mill. Do you hear me? Ah am the master of this family and Ah will not, will never allow such a thing. Instead, ye can do as Ah suggested right at the start of this discussion ... tell Kate the true state of things here, let her remove the rose-tinted spectacles and allow her to dig deep into her obviously well-filled purse. Ye will do as Ah say, and that's final."

Chapter 7

With Jenny's adamant refusal either to tell Kate of the full extent of their plight or – even worse – to ask her for money, handouts, or help of any kind, there the matter had rested. However, Jenny's evasion that despite Hamish's 'bit of an accident at the mill' they were managing 'just fine' at Bramble Cottage, turned out not to be quite so much of a lie. Amazingly, quite out of the blue Hamish discovered a long hidden talent. Being left-handed had always been an oddity at the mill, so the loss of his right arm was less of a disadvantage to him than it would have been for a right-handed man. Even with only the use of his one remaining hand and some help from Jenny in setting up small vices to hold the articles for him, he had something of a flair for designing trinkets, ornaments, and even small pieces of jewellery made from seashells, semiprecious stones, and even the artistic driftwood to be found on the many beaches of the Island of Bute.

Jenny, remembering Kate's talent for finding ways of making money, took some of Hamish's products to a small shop in Montague Street that sold souvenirs to the tourists and summer visitors. The proprietor Mr Frame agreed to take the trinkets on consignment and sell them, charging a small commission. Sales were good enough that Mr Frame decided to buy Hamish's future output to prevent any competitors sharing the market. To Jenny's surprise he also made the suggestion that if Jenny could provide knitted or sewed goods he would buy those too. Despite Hamish's diatribe about Jenny taking a job, knitting or sewing for Mr Frame was quite acceptable.

So successful and plentiful became their output in a few short months that Hamish and Jenny discovered to their amazement they had something of a cottage industry. With the making and selling of such little souvenirs of one kind or another, to the growing and ever increasing number of holiday visitors, they had money enough for food to keep body and soul together ... and perhaps even more importantly for Hamish to enable them to hold their heads high with the dignity of their labour in the local community. With the range of their well-made goods now making a brave display in Mr Frame's wee shop in Montague Street, there was much local admiration for the way in which both Jenny and her man had overcome their troubles, bad luck which would have beaten into the ground of poverty a less enterprising couple.

The way Jenny told it all to Kate in her letters, it was as if the mishap at the mill had actually turned out to be the best thing that could possibly have ever happened to them. With both husband and wife being busy and fully occupied with their respective chores, yet again and far beyond their wildest dreams, a measure of peace and contentment descended on the cottage. Friends came and went, church soirees were attended, the Minister when he called was entertained to tea in the best front room as was the well established local custom. Day by day Gordon and Glen grew more independent, more able to stand up for themselves, but nevertheless very wary of their still jealous but now rather more restrained and better supervised step-sister.

One thing that never changed was Jenny's delight in the weekly letter from her mother. The arrival of the news-filled letter from Kate with details of her activities over in Ireland was still the highlight of Jenny's week.

One morning, with Postie's usual cheery wave, he came into the kitchen, enjoyed a cup of tea and a pancake with Hamish and Jenny, then before setting out again on the rest of his rounds, he handed over the always eagerly awaited letter. With a happy smile on her face, Jenny had took herself off into the best front room, there to digest in peace and quiet Kate's latest ourpourings.

Dearest Jenny,

It was lovely to get all your latest news and hear again that something good has indeed triumphed over something bad. As you so rightly say, that slight mishap at the mill has obviously proved to be a blessing in disguise. You know, my dear, life is like that ... as long as you face problems with courage, fortitude, and a positive attitude you can always extract something of value from whatever upsets life can throw. If I have managed to get that message over to you in the years of your growing up ... and it would seem that's another of life's hard-won lessons you have now learned for yourself ... then perhaps I might be allowed to congratulate myself that despite our hardships in the past, I did after all manage to bring you up to be a decent human being and a responsible, caring citizen of whatever community you happen to be in.

Anyway, I'll get down from my soapbox now, dearest. You have never actually mentioned exactly what happened to Hamish in his accident, but I gather it could not have been anything too drastic, especially since you have been coping so successfully with your very own little cottage industry for the ever expanding holiday souvenir market. Mind you, having said that, I must admit I had a quiet smile at the very idea of your once again making crocheted matinee and bed-jackets. Not but what you've always been something of an expert with your crochet hook and knitting needles, but like me, I'm sure you'll remember that famous, or should I say infamous, time when you virtually welded the edges together with a decorative fringe. Now as we both know, that would have been a major economic disaster for the Kinnon household then, but between us, we talked our way out of it, didn't we, dear?

The news from here is: life continues to be good. In fact, I would even go so far as to say one way another, it is little short of a dream come true. Terence is the best husband in the world, we are so very happy together and he is forever telling me I was destined to be the Lady of the Big House, because I carry off the role as to the manner born.

Bridget my cook/housekeeper, the four housemaids, the gang of garden boys, and the general factotum Murphy (I refuse to call him anything so grand as a butler) are all really first class. Right from the very start, bless them, they, one and all, accepted me in the role into which my marriage to my dear Terence propelled me.

It is strange being here, close to where I was born. Not all that far from Laggan House that Pearce and I fled from all those years ago. I now find that Pearce wasn't the eldest son after all – the one Danny referred to as Uncle Desmond was the heir. Pearce wouldn't have inherited Laggan House or the family money, so my marriage to him hadn't cost him his heritage after all. He would have had to make his own way in the world as the younger son and I wonder if he would have made any better a job of it without me. Somehow I doubt it. No one round here remembers me and certainly no one associates me with the lady's maid that ran off with one of the sons of Laggan House. Desmond Kinnon is now nearly seventy-one – just short of a year older than Pearce would be if he had lived – and when he goes there will be no one left at the House that would remember the old scandal. His son, who now lives in Dublin, will be the new owner.

You know, I sometimes wonder in odd moments what my staff would make of it if they knew of my past history. I don't suppose that too many ladies of the manor have, like me, risen from being a lowly kitchen skivvy, lady's maid, rag-picker, cleaner, seamstress, waitress at a workmen's restaurant, and manageress of an Irish Navvies' Hostel. Still, that's all in the past and as they say, the past is another country, so perhaps best left there and not visited in memory too often.

Anyway, to turn to another matter, I had a long letter from your brother the other day. He and his wife and bairn have now settled well over in Canada. Yes, I do know you and Danny never really got on all that well together, but having said that, at least you finally did part company as friends, so that's something I suppose, and one reason as to why I thought you possibly might be interested to have news of him from time to time. As you already know, they accepted with a glad heart some of the acres of free land out on the Prairies which were at the time being offered to those immigrants brave enough to accept the challenge of such a pioneering new life. Although they had a horrendous voyage outward bound from Greenock on one of those terrible but well-named coffin ships, they did survive and also weathered the initial hardships of the Canadian winters out in the wilderness beyond Winnipeg. But now, they're well settled on their homestead and the latest good news is they are again expecting a new arrival. In case you might like to crochet or knit a gossamer wedding-ring shawl for the new baby when it comes, please let me know and I'll forward Danny's address to you. I feel it would be a lovely gesture to send such a gift to Danny and his wife and I do hope you will agree. After all, with all the awful things happening in the world today, I think we should all remember no matter what past differences there may have been within our own ranks, it is always good to mend fences and keep up family contacts. And I do feel a beautiful wedding-ring gossamer shawl, created with your own fair hands, would help cement family ties and would obviously be appreciated when sent across those thousands of miles to keep a tiny new baby cosy and warm in the depths of a Canadian winter. Anyway, that's the suggestion, so I'll leave it with you, Jenny.

Well, seems to me that I've rambled on quite long enough in this letter, so now it only remains to send lots of love from Terence and me to you, Hamish and your dear wee family. Come to think of it, why should I stop at saying merely 'lots of love' when what I really mean is we both send you all the love in the world. Your ever-loving Mammy and Terence.

P.S. You asked about that recent heart scare I had. Well, I must admit that I do still feel very tired ... I think we Scots tend to call the feeling 'a wee thing wabbit', but otherwise, I do assure you, I'm just perfectly fine. And with Terence looking out for me and my staff ... there I go again boasting ... my staff waiting hand-n-foot on me, what right do I have to feel tired? Ridiculous, isn't it? After all, let's face it, tiredness was what I did know all about in the old days when I was holding down two or three wee jobs all at once ... washing communal stairs, cleaning other folk's houses, washing dishes at Mac's, and sewing garments till midnight ... all in a bid to keep the family fed and clothed. Now, that was tiredness! But as I believe they sometimes say about the Royal Family's health, 'no further bulletins', and that's the way I'd like it too. After all, like everybody else, at forty-eight, I too am getting on a bit in years but not I hasten to say as yet 'going doon the brae', to coin yet another famous Scots phrase. Now that really is all for this letter ... or should I say given the length of it, this novel.

Much love, Mammy.

Chapter 8

When later that same evening Jenny discussed and read out Kate's latest letter to Hamish, he listened carefully, digesting its contents, before finally saying: "Oh, so I gather that even after all this time, ye never did tell Kate the full extent of my injuries from that accident at the mill?"

Jenny nodded her assent but beyond that made no comment, sensing and fearing that it was the onset of yet another marital row. When she again raised her head, it was to see Hamish, a quizzical expression on his face, studying her.

"Mind ye, there's one thing Ah must say. Upon reflection, Ah'm now damned glad ye didnae enlighten her to the full picture. And especially now that we're making such a success of our wee souvenirs business. We've achieved that by ourselves. No, ye were right, Jenny, it would never have done for me to have gone cap in hand, putting on a poor mouth to yer rich relatives."

In her eagerness to reply, Jenny leant forward until their faces were almost touching. Unable to resist the temptation to say, 'I told you so', she wagged a mischievous finger in his face and said: "That's all very fine now, Hamish, but don't let us ever forget that it was you who first suggested once we should have asked Kate and Terence for monetary help ... and as for ..."

Hamish silenced her with a look.

"Dae Ah really hae to spell it out to ye, Jenny? Dae ye no recognise an apology even when it is being thrust in yer face? Listen, Jenny, my wee lamb, things are going well for us now so why dinnae we follow yer Mammy's excellent advice about putting past differences behind us, eh no? After all, and Ah'm sure even ye would agree with this, in the horrendous aftermath of yon accursed accident, we both said things we really didnae mean, all in the white heat of the moment. That's a fact, is it not?"

As her husband finished speaking, the tears were already trickling down Jenny's face. Even so, she managed to say: "Hamish, do you really mean it? Forgive and forget, is that it?"

Hamish nodded soundlessly as the emotion of the moment seemed in danger of engulfing him. Then, with a supreme effort of will, he adopted an impish grin on his face and whispered: "Just one other thing in the letter. There was some mention of a wedding-ring gossamer shawl for a baby. Just what in God's name is that when it's at home?"

Jenny wiped away the last of her tears, laughed and said: "It's a woman's thing, Hamish. The test of a really expert knitter ... to knit a baby's shawl of such spider's-web-like fragility that it can easily be pulled through a wedding ring. Anyway, my man, if there's one thing you will not need to bother about, it's a baby's shawl; Theresa and the twins are all long past that stage and anyway ...."

Hamish interrupted the flow of her words, laying a hand on her arm. "True enough, Ah don't need to have any truck with a baby's shawl. But, who knows, my bonnie Jenny, who knows but what such a delicate garment might well figure large in yer future."

Jenny gasped and blushed at the implication behind his words but Hamish had not yet finished speaking.

"Aye, it seems to me that ye and me have a deal of making up to do, and we both ken the easiest, most pleasant way of doing that, don't we?"

Even without the utterance of the crude Scottish word for the act, whether in or out of the marriage bed, the look of longing, lust and hunger in her husband's eyes said it.

Matching his mood, Jenny giggled and said: "Happen you're

right, Hamish. Maybe I should knit such a shawl for Danny's coming bairn. After all, I suppose it would be grand practice for later on … after all, as you so rightly say, we have a deal of making up to do."

By way of reply, Hamish rose to his feet, turned off the oil lantern, then held out his hand to lead Jenny over to the wall bed with its patchwork quilt. His voice husky with emotion, he said: "Seems to me ye'll have plenty of news for yer next letter to Kate."

Jenny had time only to say that she did not tell her Mammy everything, before her words were lost in his kiss.

The safe arrival of a baby girl – and a Brandane to boot – the requisite nine months later was greeted with unrestrained joy in the Darroch family. The only possible exception to the general euphoria was Theresa, now nine, almost ten, whose every action spoke louder than words … yet again her nose had been put out of joint with the arrival of the latest rival for the affection of her mother and step-father. However, given the bitter experience of virulent jealousy in full flight, this time Jenny and her husband were not only more alert to any possible danger signals, they were also more closely attuned to Theresa's needs, actions, and wildly alternating mood swings.

Chapter 9

The Monday morning in early March, 1908, had started out well enough in their now fairly well ordered routine. Jenny had waved Hamish off at the door, and saw him wend his way down the path trundling his little handcart, piled high as usual with the latest supply of their handmade goods. As was the normal weekly routine, this consignment was bound for Mister Frame and his wee shop in Montague Street right in the centre of Rothesay. Thanks to the variety, quality, and ingenuity of the range of souvenir items still being churned out by Jenny and Hamish, this now meant that Mister Frame's modest single-door shop had nowadays the look of a developing emporium and had even become something of a mecca for locals, holidaymakers and day trippers alike.

The arrangement, worked out amicably over the course of the last couple of years, well suited both parties concerned and if it was not exactly either high finance nor even accepted business practice, that was strictly between Hamish and the now bowed and rheumatic Kirkman Frame. Jenny smiled happily and hummed a wee tune to herself, secure in the knowledge that with today's consignment of goods, delivered and paid for, that was another week's food for the family safely in view. She watched Hamish as he struggled with the difficult, one-armed management of the little hand cart, and with a last wave, which her husband might or might not see, she wheeled back into the room.

With the twins and Theresa at school, and Morag still asleep in her bed, for once Jenny had the house to herself. She was enjoying this luxury to the full, and even with the day's darg of housework still to be tackled, she felt not a single twinge of guilt at quite deliberately prolonging this unexpected treat of perfect peace and an entire morning to herself. On the point of settling down with yet another mug of sweet tea, she raised her head at the imagined sound. A quick glance at Morag snuggled into the wall-bed and, save for her downy cheeks, all but invisible beneath the patchwork quilt, was enough to assure Jenny that her golden-haired bairn was still fast asleep. Then with the sound of the door sneck, closely followed by the obligatory and traditional call of, "Yoo-hoo, it's only me," Jenny's friend and neighbour Sandra Spence entered the room.

Catching sight of Jenny still standing over the patchwork-quilt-enveloped mound in the wall-bed, Sandra at once put her hands to her mouth in a highly dramatic silencing movement. Then with a comical turkey trot, Sandra advanced to the bedside where the two women, like some captive audience, gazed down in wonder and love at the angelic sleeping child.

"Uch, Jenny, she's a right wee darlin'. The wee soul, would ye just look at her. Suckin' away at her wee thumb. Honest tae God, it's fair cheered me up just looking at the wee pet, God love her. The only pity is that they grow up."

The adoration session over for the time being and with Jenny's dream of a quiet morning all to herself now in shreds, Jenny pinned the requisite socially happy face on to what she was sure must so far have appeared less than welcoming, and waved her friend to the best seat by the fireside. That done, in no time at all, the two women were settled comfortably with mugs of tea and one of the soda scones, a plateful of which Sandra had deposited on the table.

As the two women chatted, joked, and exchanged news and titbits of local gossip, all the while Jenny had the feeling that nevertheless her friend was somehow skirting round the one topic which she really wanted to discuss. With a flash of instinct doubtless based on their years of friendship and Jenny's own knowledge of Sandra's domestic circumstances, suddenly all was clear. As their shared laughter died away over the latest anecdote about the newly arrived from the mainland youngish Minister, a rather wan, wild-eyed, and haunted-looking individual, yet still the target and would-be social conquest of every mother on the Island of Bute with a drab and unlovely spinster-of-the-Parish daughter in tow, a silence fell on the two friends.

The silence grew to the point where Jenny finally leant across and, laying a hand on her friend's arm, she said: "Somehow I get the feeling it isn't really the baldie-heided Meenister, the eternal bachelor we're talking about, now is it, Sandra?"

At once Sandra's eyes clouded over and it was a moment or two before she could trust herself to speak. When the hard-won words did come and the sorry tale was told and Sandra's latest domestic turmoil was laid bare in all its misery, Jenny at first sat in silent contemplation of what had just been revealed to her. At a loss to know how best either to comfort or even in any way help her friend, Jenny took the tried-and-tested way out.

"Another wee cup of tea, Sandra? I'll make a fresh pot while you check up on Morag for me. Then we'll get down to business, for there has to be a way out of this. And you know what they do say about two heads being better than one and that with effort, it is always possible to extract something good from something bad."

Half an hour or so later, they were still deep in ideas, suggestions, self-help cures and an even greater in-depth discussion, all of which somehow just led them back, more frustrated and puzzled than ever, right back to where they had started.

Sandra mopped again at her red-rimmed eyes and said: "Uch, don't get me wrong. Fine well I do know that Robb's a good man. He worships the weans, and in the usual way, the only time he ever takes a bucketful is when the drams of whisky are flowing at Hogmany. He's certainly no like some of the drunken eejits we

could both name that stoat aboot this Island. But you see, it was
losing his job like that and all so sudden. He's been working at the
Red Shed Boatyard man and boy, aw his days. But times is hard.
And it's no even his boss's fault, for he himself must be struggling
with little or no money coming in. He didnae want tae give Robb
the sack, for after all these years, fine well he knows what a good
worker my man is, but what else could he dae? And God knows
how we'll survive! Still an all I know he'll probably get wee odd
jobs and aw that but without a fixed weekly amount coming in,
how am Ah going tae feed the weans?"

Jenny nodded but made no comment, sensing as she did there
was more Sandra wanted to get off her chest.

"If ye must know, what really upset me and got me going like,
it was this morning, seein' yer ain good man setting off aw jacose-
like wi his wee handcart piled high wi your homemade goods.
Weel, suddenly it aw just hit me, dawned on me what dire straits
ma Robb and me's in. Poor Robb, nae work, nae money comin' in
and he hasnae even got so much as a handcart tae his name. What
a bloody life, eh?"

Sitting in silent contemplation for a few more minutes, Jenny
suddenly raised her head. She knew, yes, and knew beyond all
doubt … yes, she had the answer. And best of all, it was one which
in time, could well benefit both their households. After all, if her
own Hamish could set up a cottage industry and he with only one
hand and still struggle in coping with his handcart then what might
a two-armed normally abstemious Robb manage to achieve over
time? Not wishing to waste a moment, lest the butterfly of such a
wonderful idea float away back to whatever realm it came from,
Jenny at once set about detailing her master plan to Sandra. By
now Sandra's eyes were shining, not this time with tears, but now
with the light of hope dawning in them.

"That's it then, Sandra, my old pal," Jenny said. "The very
minute Hamish gets home this afternoon I'll have a word with him

and, knowing how well the two men already get on, he's bound to agree to such a scheme."

Just then the door burst open and a clearly whisky-fuelled Hamish stumbled into the room together with the words: "Ah'm back earlier than Ah said, but something's happened. Jenny, ye're no going tae believe this. Just wait till Ah tell ye what's happened noo."

He saw Sandra. "Oh, it's yersel, Sandra. That's lucky. Mr Frame wis on aboot model boats again and ye ken Ah'm no really good at them. He fair went on aboot them and how he could sell as many as we could make, and if we couldnae make him some he'd need tae find somebody that could. Well, Ah wis a bit put oot and popped intae the pub … jist for a wee shot tae help me think, ye ken … and Ah bumped intae Robb. Ah telt him aboot the boats and ye'll never guess what he said."

Hamish didn't wait to hear if Jenny and Sandra had any guesses. "Robb said he wis a dab hand at the hulls and the like but he could never get aw the riggin' and the sma twiddly bits like the painting an such jist right. Ah kin dae thae twiddly bits! Robb's away hame tae tell his missus – oh, that's ye, Sandra and yer right here – Robb and me are going tae make some boats and get them doon to Frame. Between us we'll make grand boats for Frame tae sell."

Hamish looked puzzled as Jenny and Sandra clung to each other, laughing.

"What are the pair o ye laughing at? It's a grand idea. Robb and me have always been pals and noo he's lost his job he'll have time to work wi me."

Chapter 10

Throughout her young life, Theresa had always loved to dance. Even as a toddler, still staggering about and teetering perilously close to steps and sidewalks, the moment she heard the slightest strains of music ... be they issuing from fiddle, piano, or even the skirl of the pipes ... then she would be transformed. Jenny had always encouraged her and many a time she would clap her appreciation of her daughter's untutored dance steps, pat her hand fondly and say: "But you're a rerr wee dancer, Theresa."

Of course, Jenny knew a half a crown a week invested in lessons from a reputable dancing teacher would not only be money well spent, it would also provide a wonderful incentive and life-enhancing experience for her daughter. However, Jenny also knew the expenditure would most certainly not end there, for in addition there would be the ongoing costs of special dance shoes, a variety of different costumes ... everything from the shamrock decorated outfit of the Irish Colleen, through the clogs and gingham apron and hat of the archetypal little Dutch girl, and on then into the even more expensive Scottish Highland Dance regalia. And with money being everlastingly in such short supply, the spiralling costs of travelling round the country in order to attend the many Scottish Dance competitions, festivals, and traditional Highland Games Days ... such an expenditure would be completely out of their league.

But lack of money or not, as the years had passed, Theresa still clung to her great love of dancing and there the matter had rested for many a long day. If Jenny were being strictly honest with herself, from time to time she did have severe pangs of guilt in that Theresa no longer even bothered to pester her for dancing lessons. But each time Theresa would launch into a completely unselfconscious dance routine of her own highly inventive composition, then Jenny would grieve and think: *If only I could ever have money and cash to spare, I'd treat that wee lamb to instruction from the best dancing teacher in the land. The wee soul, it's all such a waste for she has a wonderfully natural rhythm and an inborn love of music.*

What made matters even worse to cope with was it was thanks only to Jenny's own fierce independence that Theresa had in fact been denied the opportunity of having lessons; and not only the lessons themselves, but also the cost of every conceivable dancing outfit known to man to be paid for her.

Jenny could still remember the content of letters from Kate on the subject. In fact, she could recall them almost word for word.

"But Jenny, why on earth won't you let me at least put something towards the bairn's future dance expenses? After all, now that I'm married to Terence, well let's just say that money is no longer a problem."

But independent to the last, Jenny would not hear of it. And despite a few tentative references to the subject in Kate's letters, all of which hints, subtle or otherwise, had been entirely ignored by Jenny, there the matter had rested. And this had been the pattern over the past few years. However, with Theresa's increasing jealousy over the new baby, Jenny noticed with some alarm that with each day, not only was Theresa becoming more and more withdrawn, she also had given up all interest in her dancing. When matters had come to a head, Jenny determined to bring everything into the open in the hope of finding some sort of solution. That very night, once the children were in bed, as Jenny and Hamish sat by the fireside, Jenny finally broached the subject.

Having heard her out, her husband sat in silence for a few minutes' contemplation.

Finally, he leant across, laid a hand on her arm and said: "Listen, ma ain darlin'. Aw thing that upsets and worries ye ... weel put it this way ... yer troubles are ma troubles. So here's what we dae ... mind ye Ah cannae afford aw that much. But having said that, Ah'm sure if we work at it, we can stretch the pennies, at least far enough tae pay for the cost of a weekly dancing lesson for the wee jealous mite. Apart from anything else, it'll make her feel that wee bit special, and then she'll no feel too much that what with the new baby and aw that excitement, that her ain nose is oot of joint. What dae ye think, darlin? Would that please ye?"

The look on Jenny's face said it all. Such a new departure for Theresa would indeed give her something else to think about. At the same time, hopefully divert her energies away from the rages and sneaky attacks, all of them expressions of her terrible jealousy so often needlessly inflicted on the twins and baby Morag.

Amazingly and almost right from the word go, the financial sacrifice of making each single penny stretch to do the work of three paid dividends. Not only was there much greater harmony in the house but a re-energised, happier and dancing Theresa had brought a new dimension into the lives of all the inhabitants of Bramble Cottage.

It was yet again approaching the month of August and as always on the Island of Bute, the nearer came the advent of Games Day then the greater grew the activity, preparation and general excitement throughout the length and breadth of 'The Madeira of Scotland'. When the big day itself arrived, the noble and well established tradition of Bute Highland Games Day launched into its usual memorable routine. The entire town was ablaze with flags, bunting, and tartan; there was hustle and bustle on all sides;

each and every shop had special, tartan bedecked Games oriented window displays; and a brisk trade in food, drink, and the essential 'watter o' life' was being carried on in all the many restaurants, tearooms, and the packed-to-capacity drinking howffs throughout the Island; there were emotive family reunions; a sea of happy smiling faces; a babble of foreign tongues, and accents from the farthest corners of Scotland; and above it all, from early light and the arrival of the first boat from the Mainland, the air was rich with the glorious, nerve-tingling, heart-tugging, weep-inducing skirl of the pipes.

This year Games Day had a special significance for the Darroch family. Theresa, having marched up to the park in company with the other pipers, dancers and competitors in the many different sporting events, newly kitted out in her hand-me-doon yet pristine Highland outfit, had danced her socks off, and came second in her own Highland dance event, that of performing a spirited Highland fling. Almost before either she or her family could realise the enormity of it all, wonder of wonder she had won a medal. Then at the end of what had been the most exciting day of her young life had come the greatest thrill of all. As a competitor – and a prize-winning one at that – she took her own rightful place in the procession which then led its way down the high street, past the ancient castle and then on to the grand triumphal march through the streets of Rothesay. What a wonderful, soul-inspiring sight it all was, that march of the massed pipe-bands, as with kilts swinging and bagpipes playing at full belt, there was hardly a dry eye within the ranks of the hundreds of spectators who lined the flag-bedecked streets. There behind the pipers who had travelled the world to get to Bute for this special day, there along with a host of other kilted dancers, marched Theresa, the hard-won medal pinned to her jacket. With the last rays of the evening sun glinting off her silver buttons, silver buckles on her shoes, and above all, sparkling like the miracle it truly was, the bright shiny new medal.

Later that same evening as the family celebrated with a special high tea at which the still kilted wee champion dancer in their ranks was the honoured and waited-upon guest, Jenny smiled across at Hamish. He for his part said not a word in reply but cocked his head and gave her a cheeky wink.

The tea party over, Jenny absolved her triumphant daughter, just this once, from clearing away, far less washing the dishes.

Enveloping her in the greatest of bear hugs, Jenny said: "Theresa, my wee love. Hamish and me, we're both that proud of you. And look at you in your lovely Highland outfit, you're a champion and take it from me, hen, such important folk are never expected to do the dishes. Anyway ..." here Jenny looked over at her husband, "anyway, I think Hamish is about to volunteer as dishwasher-in-chief for tonight. Is that no right, Hamish?"

At his anguished and exaggerated cry together with the mental image of her stepfather, a douty Scotsman, doing such menial work – always the province of the women of the household in Scotland – Theresa burst out into a fit of the giggles. So it was amid a welter of family unity, wild hilarity and general satisfaction in a day's work well done that Theresa's first ever dance medal was displayed in all its glory and given pride of place on top of the sideboard. One way and another, it had been quite a day.

Chapter 11

By October of 1912, now a bright pupil in second year at the local Rothesay Academy, Theresa was already showing talent in the writing of her school essays and even the occasional letter to her Granny Kate in Ireland.

As Jenny pored over her mammy's latest epistle, she worried that, bright pupil or not, Theresa seemed once again restless and unhappy, and with the exception of her writing not at all keen on school.

My Dearest Jenny,

Here's another five pager about to wing its way to you. As always I enjoyed your latest newsy letter and I was overjoyed at how well everything is going for you and Hamish. How time flies. It seems just the other day I was reading of the arrival of Morag and now your news of her is full of the adventures of a sturdy four-year-old.

So Theresa is settling in well at second year at Rothesay Academy, is she? It will be no time at all until she is a young lady and striking out with her own goals in life, for the years go past so very quickly. Mind you, I must say, I was a wee bit concerned about the fact of her ongoing jealousy and backbiting with regard to the rest of the family. Of course, we do all know who she takes that aspect of her character from, don't we? With the passage of the years, you may well have very conveniently forgotten, but I never, ever forget. Just how jealous ... indeed I would almost be tempted to say insanely jealous ... you were of Danny. You always held to the view, and said so in no uncertain terms that you regarded 'Danny boy' as my own particular favourite and that being so you invariably considered yourself to be something of an outsider. No matter how I tried to convince you otherwise, you would have none of it.

Please do believe me, I loved you all equally, but if you were determined to ignore that fact, what more could I possibly have done, other than keep on bestowing on you all the motherly love of which I was capable? But one thing I will say in my own defence; if I did appear to favour Danny unduly, that was just due to my perhaps overcompensating him for the terrible ill-feeling – perhaps even hate would not be too strong a word – that existed between poor Danny and his father. So there you have it, Jenny, if Theresa is of a jealous nature, then let's face it, she must take that particular facet of her character from you.

Now then, if you are still reading this letter even after such a harangue of home truths, please let me now turn to a much more pleasant aspect of Theresa's nature and inborn talents. You mentioned recently that her teachers up at the Academy are loud in their praise of her essays and her knowledge of and keen interest in literature and all aspects of the written English language. From what you say and from such excellent school reports, she would most definitely have a leaning and talent towards the career of being a writer, a poet of distinction, or perhaps even a teacher of English. As I remember, you yourself were set on being a teacher and I for one know that you most certainly had the brains to have followed through successfully on such an ambition, had your life been allowed to turn out differently. Of course, while I have no wish ever to speak ill of the dead ... it was your late-lamented father who put the hems on any such otherwise attainable ambitions. Anyway, I'm not really wanting to rake over old family rows and upheavals; what I'm trying to say is this ... you yourself were in fact, and indeed still are, a very brainy scholar. So that's something else that Theresa obviously inherited from your side. That being so, Jenny, do please encourage her in every way, won't you? Do that and I'm sure with having her mind fully occupied with the development of her writing, she will have less time or inclination to indulge in jealous feelings, rages or spiteful actions of any kind. And of course whatever other interests she might have, be it in music, dance, gardening, or whatever, I know I can trust you to help her gain the fullest enjoyment and interest from such activities.

As for me, my own wonderful life in Ireland goes on apace, with Terence being as caring, attentive and loving as always. He is also a marvellous employer and our recent farewell party for a long-serving housemaid who was leaving to get married was a huge success.

Next time, lots more news to share with you. Meanwhile, do please give my love to your dear self, Theresa, Hamish, Glen, and Gordon ... and not forgetting Theresa's current arch-rival, wee baby Morag.

Lots of love from, Your ever-loving Mammy, Terence, and our own latest arrival ... our new wee puppy, Towser.

PS: I meant to say how delighted I am to hear that you and Danny are now in fairly regular touch with your letters across all those miles to the Canadian Prairies. The gift of that exquisite shawl for their own wee Katie most certainly did help mend fences. And wasn't it lovely that they chose to call the new baby after me ... I can't tell you how delighted I was. Oh, oh I do hope that doesn't sound as though I had been expecting you to call your new arrival after me as well, for that has never been my intention. I do think it was a lovely gesture to call your wee one after Hamish's dear departed Granny, since she too had been a born and bred Brandane and I do know what store people on your lovely Island set by that.

PPS: Don't think I'm getting big-headed, but maybe Theresa takes some of her writing ability from me ... I seem to recall that at one point of my own varied lifetime experience, I was something of a poet ... a published one at that! So there now, what do you think of that, Jenny? On that final note, I'll close and, of course, I'll be writing to you soon again.

Love, much love, Mammy.

Chapter 12

With each summer that came, so too did the holidaymakers, and as they flocked to the Island in ever-increasing numbers, this meant that business was booming for Hamish and Jenny. Since they had combined forces and pooled their talents with Sandra and Robb some four years ago, the range of souvenirs had not only widened in scope but each and every item they produced was always much in demand.

Of particular interest were the models of ships, houses and country cottages, and the smaller knicknacks and assorted fripperies decorated with intricate pokerwork. Many a returning holidaymaker, on the way back to the grime, slavery, and smoke of Glasgow's hundreds of manufactories would be clutching at least one of these reminders of happy days spent in Royal Rothesay.

In common with many families on the Island who opened their doors and spread out the welcome mat to summer visitors, Jenny and Hamish would move themselves and their children out to live in the garden shed, or better still to any available out-house when necessary. This was especially so for the duration of the annual Glasgow Fair when rented accommodation on the Island was at a premium.

So the month of July, 1913, was no exception, and Jenny enlisted the help, albeit grudgingly given, of Theresa in order to move some of the family's goods and essential chattels out to the shed in readiness for what the Scots always chose to call 'the flittin'.

As mother and daughter worked away together in what was little short of a sulky silence on one hand, and the feelings of an outraged housewife on the other, Theresa suddenly downed tools and whined: "Listen, Mum, I don't see why the twins can't help us with this. Yes, I do know that Morag's still too wee to be of much help. But what about the twins? Surely the boys are now old enough and ugly enough, at least to do a spot of lifting? It beats me why you and me should be the only ones doing any of the hard graft. It's the same story every year."

Jenny straightened up her aching back and pushed a stray lock of hair safely back into its pin-enmeshed nest. Then and only then did she look at her first born, albeit more in sorrow than in anger.

"Uch, Theresa … you're not getting started on all this jealousy carry-on yet again, are you? Fine well you know if anyone benefits from the extra money in catering for the with-attendance summer visitors, then it's you. Just don't you ever forget that it helps to pay for your dancing lessons … not to mention all those fancy outfits for the competitions. And, quite apart from that consideration, the extra money in hand also means that you can get the chance of staying on at school a bit longer. And that in turn means that rather than having to go into some dead-end job at the mill, like so many of your classmates have had to do already, you are being presented with untold opportunities for a better future."

Theresa, determined to have none of it, flung down the handful of cutlery she had been in the process of gathering together. With an angry cry, she rounded on her unsuspecting mother and yelled: "Mum, for goodness' sake. Fine well you know I've always hated being the odd one out in any given situation. Rather than having to stay on extra years at any old school, I'd much rather be the same as all the rest of my pals."

Jenny gave vent to her feelings as, with a hefty bang, she slammed down a stack of cooking pots, one of which, in keeping with her mood of utter frustration, then toppled over and crashed onto the kitchen floor with a noise fit to awaken the dead.

"Theresa, you ungrateful girl. How dare you even think such thoughts, far less put them into words. When I think of the sacrifices we are making and all for the sake of letting you get extra years of schooling. Education! Hmph! Just wasted, completely thrown away on a spoiled, selfish, ungrateful brat like you. Just you wait till Hamish hears about this latest ploy of yours. I can tell you right now ... he will not be amused."

"But Mum, I still don't want ..."

Having turned away from her in disgust, Jenny now wheeled back round to face her daughter. With a face like thunder she shouted: "But Mum nothing! Listen, I don't give a single damn what you want or don't want. Not any more, my girl. God Almighty, when I was young, I'd have given just about anything for the opportunity you've been handed on a plate ... an opportunity you seem hell-bent on destroying."

Since there was no answer that Theresa could possibly offer without being shot down in flames, she kept her silence. Thus it was left to Jenny who, with a final defiant chucking of the nearest wash-cloth, shouted out: "Right, my girl, that's more than enough of all this. We've got work to do. And before you get off on your high horse yet again, listen to me and listen to me well, for I'll not say this again ... No! The boys will not be helping. This is women's work. And let's face it, my dear girl, when did you ever see any Scotsman worthy of the name so much as lifting a duster to help around the house? Anyway, the twins have something much more manly and more important to do this day ... they're scheduled to go along to the drill hall to join in a pipe band practice, for the Games come the month of August."

Even as Jenny said the words, she knew in her heart of hearts that the same proviso could well have applied to Theresa since she too would have to get in quite a bit of extra rehearsing for the highland dance competitions at the same Bute Highland Games. However, as she had said, perhaps that too was women's work, so no apology nor further explanation would be called for. Even so, being on the side of women herself and perhaps even to salve her conscience a little, Jenny crossed the room, tip tilted the still scowling face of her daughter and said: "Listen, hen, once we've got this chore done, how's about you and me sitting down to a cuppa and one of Sandra's treacle scones. Then between us three women we'll start on making you a braw new white blouse for your outfit, one with a lovely lace jabot, eh no? After all, that's women's work as well ... and while we're at it, we can all have a real good blether. Don't forget, darlin', there are aye some compensations tae make up for being of the female species."

As Jenny watched the scowl on her daughter's face disappear like magic to be replaced by the broadest of grins, she thought, *Aye, it's a pity that Hamish couldnae have watched all this performance, he'd have been right proud of me. He's right enough, I do seem well able to relate to youngsters. Anyway, the crisis seems to be over for the moment.*

And there the matter had rested with not another word on the subject being uttered either by Jenny or her firstborn. Even so, and as always, Jenny poured out all the details in a long letter to Kate ... not that she expected her mother over in Ireland to resolve the situation in any practical way, but at least she herself felt the better of having confided in someone who was sufficiently far removed and therefore not really involved in the immediate problem.

Chapter 13

It was a couple of weeks later and as Jenny read Kate's lengthy reply to her own recent catalogue of moans and miseries about Theresa, her eyes widened in amazement. Not sure that she had fully understood Kate's suggestion – so earthshakingly original was it – she sat down to reread the document and hopefully this time to digest fully the letter's contents.

My Dearest Jenny,

Since you are obviously so concerned about Theresa's attitude, her current difficult behaviours, and her total aversion to higher education of any sort, I'll now come straight to the point. It's a strange old world, isn't it dear? Just think, all those years ago you yourself would have given the world for just such an opportunity as your own daughter is now spurning. Yes, your own ambition was to stay on at school and later on really make something of your life, but no, that was not allowed to happen. I'm sure you know, but if you don't already know, then let me tell you now … I myself still grieve sore that the additional education which you so desperately craved was denied you. Hold on, I said I would get straight to the point and instead of that, here I am wandering down the dark and probably best hidden wynds and alleys of memory lane. Aye, that's all in the past and that's the best place to leave it all.

So, let's now see how we can solve the present crisis, for crisis it is when dealing with any young person's future, especially more so when Theresa is my adored granddaughter and your currently rather troubled first born. The crux of the matter is that since reading your letter, I have given this whole situation a great deal of thought. And also, now I do hope you won't mind this, but Terence and I have night after night discussed it at length. The solution may or may not be a happy or acceptable one to you, but one thing is sure ... it will most certainly astound you. So, here goes, Jenny, here is precisely what Terence and I would suggest ...

The letter ran on for another four pages. By the end of that morning, Jenny felt that not only did she know their contents by heart, but she could have quoted them chapter and verse at the drop of a hat and have been word perfect.

Even so, she knew that before anything else could happen, she must discuss the matter in its entirety with Hamish, at the soonest possible moment. And much as she could hardly contain her impatience, she knew that she must choose her moment carefully. That being so, she then bustled around the kitchen in preparing his favourite meal of mince-n-tatties knowing full well that the way to a man's heart, not to mention his best possible humour, lay in first of all providing his stomach with a gutful of satisfying food. Having prepared the meal, all that then remained was to give him lavish helpings when he came in from his workshop at noon, a relatively quiet time in the Darroch household with only wee Morag home and Theresa and the boys safely eating their lunchtime bread and cheese on the seafront at Rothesay before returning to school for the afternoon session.

Hamish laid down his cutlery, gave a satisfied nod of his head, patted his ample stomach and said: "My, that was just grand, Jenny."

Jenny nodded, suggested to Morag that she should go outside to play and was on the point of producing Kate's letter when

Hamish, obviously with an eye to the main chance, decided to push his luck that little bit further.

"Jenny. Did Ah hear ye mention mibbe a wee cuppa tea and a bit o yer shortbread ... just tae finish off with, ye ken."

Biting her lower lip with impatience, Jenny said not a word but duly produced the requested tea and sweet bite. She then waited with what patience she could muster until Hamish had finished eating. Then at last, at long last and with the dishes cleared off the table, she produced the letter from Ireland. As he read on through the bulky epistle, Hamish's eyebrows rose higher and higher with amazement, until Jenny was convinced that he now looked as astounded as she herself had felt on first reading her mother's letter. So with that in mind and, as if instructing a not very bright, not quite twenty shillings to the pound pupil, Jenny then took the letter from him and laying it aside, proceeded to take him verbally through the details yet again. Knowing it all by heart as she now did, she went through the earthshaking suggestion as if by rote.

No sooner had she finished than Hamish sat back in his chair, ran his fingers through his unruly waves, let out a long sigh of amazement and said: "Would Kate really do that? Go to such lengths? Jenny, honestly, I just don't know what to say about ..."

His wife smiled fondly. "Well, suppose you let me do the talking, Hamish. But first of all, what about another cup of tea and mibbe even a sliver of yon millionaire's shortbread I've been saving for a special occasion. How would that suit you, dear?"

Hamish's grin was answer enough to indicate that such a treat would in fact suit him very well thank you, before they would finally get down to discussing the nitty-gritty and the finer details of Kate's involvement in Theresa's future.

It was some half hour or so later when Jenny again broached the subject.

"Like I said earlier Hamish, let me do the talking. After all, I am her mother and there is one other matter you may have overlooked in the excitement of the moment. Let us not forget after all, it isn't even as if you ever did get around to legally adopting Theresa, now is it?"

Hamish flinched, taking Jenny's comment as a rude reminder and indeed a curt criticism of his own past conduct, or in this case, his lack of it, and his weakness of moral fibre in not following through on his previously given and loudly voiced promise and intention to adopt Theresa as his own child. So, it was a visibly flustered and uncomfortable man who gazed across at his wife and said: "Uch, Jenny, is that no just a wee bit below the belt? After all, as God is my witness and my hand to Heaven, I honestly did mean to consult a lawyer about the legalities of all that adoption business. But you know as well as I do, somehow after my accident at the mill, well I never did get sufficiently motivated to put any such legal wheels in motion. Apart from anything else, we had barely enough money to put food on the table with which to fill our bellies, far less to fork out money for lawyers and their ilk. So if we're being totally honest, I suppose you could say that one way and another, yes, I lost the moment. And that's the top and bottom of the situation."

There was a silence between them, an almost physical silence that could be felt as they each relived their own private memories of that dreadful time when it seemed that their world had come crashing down around them. Finally, Jenny, knowing full well how very much she had hurt Hamish with her careless comment, leant forward and in a gesture of reconciliation which spoke volumes more than any words could possibly have done, she placed a hand on his cheek.

"Uch, Hamish, don't take on so, laddie, you know I wouldn't hurt you for the world. But at the risk of again opening an old wound, there is one thing I must say ... the point is this ... Kate has suggested that with there always having been a special bond between herself and Theresa, well why not allow her and Terence to legally adopt the girl?"

Rather than again enter into a dispute with Hamish, Jenny then hurried on: "And let's be sure on one point. Theresa obviously feels and in fact has already made up her mind to the fact, that as far as she is concerned, her schooldays are over. Children can leave when they're twelve, and she's thirteen past and had a full year at the Academy. Her friends are already out of school or are about to leave. Well, so be it, for with the big house to run, it does seem that without the benefit of higher education of any kind, Theresa could be kept fully employed in some capacity or other."

Alternatively, and knowing of Theresa's love of writing, Kate has suggested that her grand-daughter could act as a sort of part-time companion to her Granny, at the same time as pursuing her literary ambitions.

Again that silence as a still smarting Hamish struggled to cope not only with such surprising news but also with the strength of his own emotions. After all, adopted or not, he still regarded her as his own lovely, talented, albeit sometimes difficult, daughter.

When the silence was in danger of going on indefinitely, Hamish finally cleared his throat and said: "Correct me if I'm wrong, Jenny, but there is one other point you've missed. Although she hasn't actually spelt it out for us, recently your Mother has been having some heart problems, right? So, no doubt she would more than welcome having Theresa to live with them. So, one way and another, it all does seem like a truly wonderful opportunity for our girl. Of course, the final decision would have to be hers, and hers alone. But if she's for it ... then personally, I don't think we should stand in her way. We do know that with the boys and Morag, poor Theresa has often felt the odd man out. But with this opportunity, she would come into her own – and that could only be for the best, eh no?"

The moment that the proposal was put to Theresa, it was immediately clear that not only did she consider it the most wonderful plan she had ever heard, she could obviously hardly contain her impatience until such times as the wheels could be put in motion. So many details had as yet to be worked out ... the how, why, when, and where of it all ... and for a time, it seemed that with each new suggestion everyone was merely going around in ever increasingly demented circles. Finally, it was another detailed letter from Kate that helped put the matter into some sort of perspective. So at last a timetable of a kind was worked out which amazingly did seem to have the added benefit of taking into consideration the needs, wishes, thoughts, and ideas of all those most closely concerned with the life-changing and undoubtedly life-enhancing project.

My Dearest Jenny and Theresa,

After our recent letters it would now seem we are all fairly well agreed on a possible – might we even say a definite – plan of action. Correct me if I'm wrong, but I rather think the way we see the situation now is this ... if you are willing, Theresa, then perhaps you could help out your mum and Hamish through their busiest season of the year with the holiday visitors until the end of the summer period. A bonus to this would be also that, come the August Highland Games Day on Bute, you would still be there to compete in your dance events ... and who knows, perhaps even win another medal, or maybe even a trophy, eh? Anyway, whatever of that, then come September instead of returning to the Academy in third year for another session, you could kiss goodbye to the formal education you obviously hate so much and instead start getting ready for your new life over here in Ireland. That means that following such a plan of action, by the month of October you'll be fully prepared, in all senses, to wave a fond goodbye to Bonny Scotland and the Island of Bute and sweet Rothesay Bay and sail across to the Emerald Isle and to the warm welcome which as you already know, so surely awaits you here in our lovely home. It all makes sense, doesn't it? Anyway, do please write as soon as possible and let us know what you think of this master plan.

Ever your loving Mother and Grandmother Kate.

As Jenny finished reading out the letter to Theresa, she thought everything had been well and truly covered. From the look on her daughter's face it was clear that Theresa was well satisfied and that really nothing else remained to be discussed. This was just as well, because as Jenny stuffed the letter back into its envelope, she was surprised to unearth an additional, but un-numbered, page. By now halfway out of the doorway, Theresa paused at her mother's exclamation of surprise, and turned to say: "What's that, Mum, did you say something?"

On the point of reading aloud to her the contents of the lengthy full page postscript, Jenny stopped as the full implication of the words sank in. She raised her head to find her daughter's still questioning eyes on her, and knowing that an answer of some sort was still required of her, she said: "No, no, it's nothing. At least nothing that won't keep. So just you get off to your dancing lesson now, dear, I'll see you later."

With Theresa gone quite happily about her business, Jenny again settled back in her chair, smoothed out the postscript page and started to re-read it ...

P.S. Jenny, one more thing, Terence has just come up with a totally unexpected but absolutely wonderful idea.

As I told you recently in another letter, although I do try not to dwell too much on my health problems, I do know now I'm that bit older – fifty-four to be exact – I am rather slowing down more than somewhat and I no longer have quite the same bursts of nervous energy as was the case in the past ... in the days when I held down several wee jobs all at the same time, in an effort to keep us all fed and clothed in the Candleriggs. Anyway, here I am drivelling on again, when what I really want to tell you about is Terence's fantastic idea which incidentally, I know you will love. But to get down to business, here is what the darling man has now suggested: He and I will travel to Scotland in time to be in Bute for the Bute Highland Games to see Theresa compete in the dancing. After that we can stay a spell and Theresa will accompany us on a little tour of Scotland before we all journey back to our house in Ireland. Don't tell Theresa this in case it doesn't come off, but I'll let you know in plenty of time so that you can arrange accommodation for Terence and me in one of the local hotels or boarding houses.

Epilogue

Ireland, Summer 1919.

As Kate hobbled into the comfortable ambience of the cosy yet wonderfully elegant morning room, Terence immediately looked up from his newspaper and smiled. Then lowering the paper to his lap, he said: "You're looking very lovely this fine morning, Kate, my darling. You know, in the years since Theresa came to stay with us, you do seem so very much better in yourself. So what I say is this ... long may that improvement last."

Kate walked slowly across the sun-filled room and, pausing only to place her walking stick on the floor by his chair, she put a hand on her husband's shoulder, gave it a gentle squeeze and said: "Now then, Terence, my lad, let's have no more of this fussing about the state of my health. You can stop all such nonsense right here and now. Do you hear me? After all, and not to put too fine a point on it, neither one of us is getting any younger. And anyway, as I've told you a dozen times already the good Doctor Flynn was well pleased with my last check-up."

Terence gave a sheepish grin, laid his paper down on a nearby chair, took off his reading spectacles and finally levering himself to his feet, he took his wife in his arms. They were still locked in this embrace when behind them the door opened and Theresa came into the room.

"Oho, I see the lovebirds are still drooling over each other. Honestly, you two, what are you like? You know there are times that I really don't know where to put myself. Talk about love's not-so-young dream."

As Kate broke free of her husband's arms, a playful smile flitted across her face, giving her momentarily the appearance of a much younger woman besotted with love. Then, tearing her eyes away from Terence's adoring gaze, she turned to her grand-daughter and said: "Jealousy will get you nowhere, my girl. And nor will any snide comments about advancing age. You'll be an old lady yourself one day. So just don't you ever forget age is something that, although unasked for, does somehow creep up on all of us."

Theresa opened her mouth to reply in the same teasing manner, but determined to have the last word, Kate got in there first.

"Anyway, Theresa my girl, let's just wait until you meet your very own knight in shining armour. Aye, let's see what happens when you meet the man of your dreams. We'll see how you go on then."

With a delighted laugh Terence said: "Well thanks, Kate. It's good to hear you say it at last, at long last. Mind you, I can't say that I've ever before been called a knight in shining armour. I've been called many a thing in my day, but never that. But I'm delighted to know ... I really am the man of your dreams. Have I got that right?"

Kate, catching his mood, so well attuned were they, gave his nearest arm a playful slap. Then pointing a mock admonitory forefinger at him said: "You're at it again, aren't you, Terence O'Neil? But if despite now being aged and decrepit ... decaying gentlefolk I believe is the correct term ... if you're still fishing for compliments, you can just stop right there and behave yourself. Just try acting your age, for you'll be getting no raft of compliments from me."

As they all laughed in easy companionship, Theresa smiled at the happy couple. "Talking of compliments, Granny Kate, and I promise you nothing to do with Terence ... but you'll never guess what has happened."

Like a pair of over excited schoolchildren, both Kate and Terence at once and almost as if on cue, entered into the innocent and harmless game of making wild absurd guesses as to what possible, or even impossible event had so recently occurred in Theresa's life. Eventually, with tears of laughter streaming down her face and holding on to the stitch in her side, Theresa said: "No, no, no! Not a single one of your improbable suggestions has come anywhere within a mile of the truth. And as for Frank Doherty, blinded by puppy love or not, he has not been singing my praises to the heavens. And if you must know, already I've told him in no uncertain terms that I'll be having none of that soppy lovey-dovey nonsense from him, big daft eejit that he is."

At this point, Terence gave a deep sigh of mock resignation. "Listen Kate, why don't you ring for Bridget to bring us in a tray of tea, biscuits, and buttered soda bread, then we can all sit down in comfort and listen to what I'm pretty sure is going to be a very long story."

It had become something of a standing joke that Theresa could never ... or more correctly, chose never, to use three words in the telling of any event where three dozen would serve her purpose better and make for a more dramatic tale.

Later that same day as Theresa sat out in the little summer house overlooking the lake, she was hard at work with notebook and stub of pencil in hand when she heard a sound which caused her to raise her head. She was in time to see her grandmother leaning heavily on her now ever-present silver-topped walking stick, making her way through the rose-scented walled garden. In her other hand and clutched tightly to her bosom for safety, Kate was carrying a ribbon-tied box.

As she came into the summerhouse, Kate first of all placed the box with precision and a certain indefinable panache on to the little marble-topped table. That arranged to her satisfaction, but still making no verbal reference to the parcel whatsoever, she then proceeded to lever her rheumatic bones down into a cane chair opposite Theresa. Then and only then did she give her grand-daughter a beaming smile and say: "Yes, after the news you gave us this morning, I rather thought I would find you in here and hard at work on your next masterpiece. Listen, my dear, we were both absolutely delighted to hear of your success. Just fancy, a well-known and highly respected publisher actually sending you an acceptance of your book of short stories. It's wonderful news, darling girl, just wonderful. Terence and I, we are both so, so pleased for you."

Theresa dimpled her delight at the praise being heaped on her, enjoying the moment to the full, and not least at being called a clever girl, despite having her years of childhood now well behind her.

"Theresa, listen, I can't tell you often enough how delighted we are. Of course, I always knew of your talent at writing ... but to achieve such success so early on in your literary career ... it's marvellous. Marvellous, there's no other word for it."

"Thank you Granny. Of course, if we're being honest, we both know who I inherited my writing ambitions from, don't we? I well remember Mummy telling me, aye she was forever telling me time and time again, she was that proud of you, Granny. She never lost an opportunity to boast of the fact that you yourself were once quite a poet. Away back in our Candleriggs days, that's right isn't it?"

Kate smiled fondly as she cast her mind back, far back in time, distance, and experience of life to those days when she herself had had her own first-ever writing success with the publication of some of her work. She again nodded thoughtfully at the same time as feeling absurdly pleased with what Theresa had just told her.

"Good gracious me. Just fancy Jenny remembering that, far less boasting about it. Yes, I suppose I was what you might call a published poet. Although, really my poem was ... well let's be honest, I suppose it was nothing other than just a sort of advertising jingle. But for all that, yes, I was fair proud of it."

As Kate sat dreamily staring into space with a faraway look in her eyes, Theresa knew better than to disturb her train of thought. This was borne out when her grandmother went on.

"My wee advertising poem, I wrote it for a Workman's Restaurant in Govan. Trade was slack, you see, and between my literary outpouring and the wee ceramic pigs holding the trays of ashet pies in the shop window ... well, it all encouraged the local people, poverty stricken or not, to come along and spend even more of their precious threepenny bits. Yes, that was Mac's Restaurant and I was a kitchen skivvy there, but amazingly, a kitchen skivvy who had actually written a poem. Oh, it's all a very long time ago, Theresa, and so much has happened since then."

Theresa closed her notebook, smiled fondly at her grandmother, then wide-eyed with surprise, said: "A kitchen skivvy indeed. Is that what you're telling me, Granny? Well, let's face it, Granny Gumdrops, you're certainly not that now, are you? Aye, no two ways about it, you've most certainly come up in the world."

Kate nodded. "That's for sure. But like I say, it was all a long time ago and as to my years in service ... well, let's just say that I've had an eventful life. Anyway, whatever of that, who knows, Theresa but what one day when you are a famous, rich and well-published author ... who knows, maybe one day when I am dead and gone you'll write the story of the Kinnons of Candleriggs. Wouldn't that be something? Aye, stranger things have happened, let's face it. Anyway, my lass, don't you ever forget that truth is stranger than fiction. Aye, that it is."

There was a shared silence between the two women as both in mind's eye tried to imagine a future, and an important future at that. And one in which a bastard child from Glasgow's Candleriggs would finally emerge as a leading light on the world's literary stage.

Kate smiled as the thought crossed her mind. *Aye, such a tale would in itself be well worth the telling. What a belter of a story that would make.* Then, giving herself a mental shake, Kate smiled across at her beloved Theresa.

"One last word ... like I say, never ever forget that truth is indeed stranger than fiction. So since you are obviously destined to become a famous author, there's one thing always to remember, my dear; you need look no further than life itself and the human condition for all the plots, intrigues, and dramas which you could possibly ever want to write about."

Having delivered herself of this monologue, Kate, all the while studiously ignoring the gift-tied box where it sat centre-stage on the little table, made as if to rise from her chair. Then, as if changing her mind, she once more settled herself against the pile of cushions. That done, she gave her granddaughter a knowing smile, together with the words: "Now then, Theresa, I know that you haven't asked. But nevertheless, I have caught you glancing once or twice at that mysterious box."

Theresa grinned. "I must admit I did rather wonder about it, especially after the pantomime production you made of it all."

"Wonder no more, my darling girl. It's for you. And I want you to open it now. Yes, rather than wait until tonight and the special dinner party, the celebration dinner which Bridget is putting on in your honour, this very night."

Needing no second invitation, her grand-daughter, curiosity fully aroused, removed the ribbon and the outer wrappings. When she lifted the lid of the rather tired-looking, travel-stained box, she caught her breath at the sight of the ornament which nestled deeply in its blue velvet lined interior. There it lay in all its fancy waistcoat finery; a ceramic pig, complete with a gaffer's little bowler hat. Hesitating as yet to remove it from its cosy bed, Theresa looked in awe at the unusual ornament. Just then Kate broke into her thoughts.

"Terence bought that for me many years ago. How on earth he

managed to run it to earth in Paddy's Market in Glasgow, I'll never know. But one thing is sure, he must have hunted it down for many a long and weary day. He knew the significance of it, you see, and I'll never ever forget the joy on his face when he finally presented it to me. In fact, in all these years, it has been my most treasured possession ... apart, of course from the engagement and wedding ring he gave me."

"Oh, Granny, I cannot possibly accept this lovely ornament, especially when it means so much to you."

"Theresa, that's the very reason I want you to have it. I'd rather see you enjoy it now than leave it to you in my will, by which time you might well have forgotten its significance."

Theresa at once laid a hand on her Granny's arm. "Oh, Granny, please, please don't even mention, far less think of such a thing as any last will and testament. I just couldn't bear it. Honestly, next thing you'll be telling me your choice of funeral hymns. Ugh! No more of such morbid talk, I'll not have it."

Kate grinned and, determined to make light of the situation, said: "Well, we'll leave it at that. Just one thing, regarding those funeral hymns ... just so long as nobody dares to sing "I Belong to Glasgow", that's my only proviso. There now, will that do you?"

Theresa smiled, glad to have put the serious subject now safely behind them. Even so, she still went on to ask her grandmother if there was anything else she should know about the history of the pig before she claimed it as her own.

Kate's eyes misted over with the remembrance. "Well, I've told you something of its pedigree already, Theresa. But since you ask, and to cut a long story short ... not something that you would ever do ... but let's just say that Master Piggie represented one of the happiest events during my dark days in Glasgow. It was thanks to him ... he inspired my writing, showed me that I was, or could be, something more than merely a kitchen skivvy, and an overworked and underpaid one at that. So, my dream now, and that of my darling Terence with whom I've discussed this, is that you should now become the proud owner of Master Piggie and that he will inspire you also. Aye, between that and our loving support behind you, we'll make a famous writer out of you yet, Theresa Kinnon O'Neil, or Theresa Darroch as you called yourself for your short story collection."

Too choked with emotion by now to say a word, Theresa instead gave her Granny the greatest of bear hugs. Then, as they disentangled themselves, she helped the old woman up from her chair, handed over her trusty walking stick and said: "Right now, Granny, Terence will be sending out a search party for us by now. Anyway, that celebration dinner you mentioned earlier ... isn't it more than high time that we were heading back into the house and getting into our glad rags?"

As the two women, arm-in-arm, strolled back to the house through the walled garden with its sweet smelling rose beds, somehow the dark days in Candleriggs might well have been lived on another planet. Despite her experiences Kate knew all too well that one way and another, her life story had been quite a journey, and often a troubled one at that, but a journey from rags to riches. But surely the richest blessing of all was the love, the deep and lasting love she had found and shared with Terence, her adored and her very own adoring husband.

As Terence greeted the two favourite women in his life with a smile and ushered them back into the welcoming warmth and comfort of the elegant drawing room for a celebratory glass of Madeira before they would all dress in best bib and tucker for the special dinner, Kate beamed with happiness. Yes, while it was true that she and Terence were getting old, and equally true that the passage of years brought in its wake the pain of aching joints, together with some loss of mobility, there were very definite compensations. She and her husband had over the years of their marriage built up a wonderful relationship, a rapport where they almost could read each others' mind and perhaps best of all, a fund of exquisite memories. *Yes,* thought Kate, *all things considered, in my long life, I have indeed been a very fortunate woman. Out of adversity and trial and tribulation, much good has come. Fate has smiled kindly on me, and I've lived life to the full and in the long run isn't that what the human experience is all about? And in taking one day at a time, Sweet Jesus, and knowing that God would always shape my back for the burden, I have weathered the storm of life to reach this wonderful haven of Ireland, the Ireland of my hopes and dreams. Who could ask for anything more? Not a single thing, unless perhaps another glass of that most excellent sherry.*

Also Available from BeWrite Books

The Kinnons of Candleriggs
by Jenny Telfer Chaplin

An uncompromising story of one woman's life in Victorian Glasgow.

Kate, a chamber maid, pregnant and unexpectedly married to the son of Irish landed gentry, expects a life fitting her husband's status, but her husband is cut off without a penny by his family. So, instead, as poverty-stricken Irish immigrants considered the lowest of the low by the Glaswegians, she has to battle religious, cultural, and social prejudice.

Told with humour, compassion, and a keen insight into the period, this is a first rate read.

Paperback ISBN 1-904492-94-9

Whispers of Ghosts
by Ron McLachlan

Up here, forget everything you thought you knew about the weather. On this mysterious yet enchanting island strange things can happen: omens, magic, restless spirits ploughing the night on their endless quest for peace, the very land and sea can speak to you of secrets, and of their very own character. When you leave, the dull ache of longing will claw in your heart drawing you back. It's a place like no other. The Isle of Arnasay.

Three generations of the Waters clan lie at the centre of this powerful tale about what happens when families and communities fall apart.

Told through the eyes of Madeline, from twenty years in the future, by which time she has become a successful, Manhattan-dwelling novelist, we are transported on a roller-coaster-like emotional voyage through the Sea Kingdoms of the Hebrides.

Steeped in Celtic, Viking, and Pictish cultural heritage, this gripping novel of close-knit family and community dynamics tells how these forces come into play and wreak havoc with the lives of the Hebrides islanders.

This tale will have meanings, echoing the harsh realities of island life, for all Gaels, at home and abroad. But its appeal goes much wider than that. You can't choose your family; all too often you can't choose your friends either. Sometimes, you can't tell the difference.

Paperback ISBN 1-904492-62-2

BeWrite Books

Also Available from BeWrite Books

Redemption of Quapaw Mountain
by Bertha Sutliff

When mountain man Beaver Mosely builds a log cabin on Blue Meadow for his bride, Keziah, it looks like the new 20th Century holds nothing but promise.

But that is before the newlyweds discover that their land is cursed - stained by the blood of an innocent Indian tribe and haunted by the ghosts of a secret and shameful past.

Bertha Sutliff brings back to life the isolated Arkansas highlands of the early 1900s and their unique people, culture and mythology in a sweeping saga of struggle and hope, love and hate, life and death ...

Paperback ISBN 1-904492-38-X

Ring of Stone
by Hugh McCracken

Two groups of teenagers – one middle-class students struggling for social justice, the other bar room toughs out for a brawl to right their own perceived wrongs – are thrust through a twist in the loop of time to the violent days of Medieval England.

Trapped in a dark era where human life is cheaper than bread and horrific torture is a popular entertainment, they find they must join forces or die.

Dogged by death every step of the way, each finds that experience of modern life has provided a skill that might – just might – save the band from an excruciating fate. And one of the group – having lost a brother to the barbaric torture death of impaling – hides a very special secret.

But as well as their own struggle for survival, the youngsters – each a convinced protestor – find themselves in a moral dilemma ... how to save their own skins whilst also fighting against the inhuman brutality and injustice suffered by new friends in a time where they don't belong.

In the latest in his popular Time Shift series, Hugh McCracken transports his readers into the harsh realities of days gone by with a unique talent for interweaving breathtaking adventure and fine historical detail.

These utterly believable pages turn faster and faster to reach an unforgettable climax as McCracken casts his spell.

Paperback ISBN 1-904224-61-X

BeWrite Books

Also Available from BeWrite Books

The Stones of Petronicus
by Peter Tomlinson

A new-born baby is left naked and exposed to die on a city wall while his father is hanged for petty theft a few feet away amid the cheers and hoots of a crazed mob.

Petronicus, an itinerant healer and man of wisdom, takes the babe to heart and together they begin a quest for knowledge, groping through a maze of magic and madness to find answers in the cruel and mysterious ancient world.

The boy grows to manhood in strange lands where a chosen few risk death in their search for truth, bitterly opposed by ruthless rulers and puppet priests who strive to enslave their subjects in a perpetual Dark Age of superstition and suspicion.

The heart-warming, honest but complex simplicity Petronicus and his adopted son share leave the reader wiser than when he joined them on their remarkable journey.

Not since the Fables of Aesop has a book like this been written. And Tomlinson wraps the sage advices in the tales Petronicus tells in a story as intriguing and exciting as any high-octane thriller - with characters so real you'll meet them time and again in your dreams ... and your nightmares.
Paperback ISBN 1-904492-76-2

Magpies and Sunsets
by Neil Alexander Marr

James McPherson has made a huge success of his new life in a new country. He has a thriving business, a wife and three daughters, a beautiful home, a public image, and a private shame.

A voice from his secret past, a voice calling from thousands of miles across the Atlantic Ocean in the thick dialect of the Edinburgh gutters haunts him.

So he returns to his native Scotland to confront his personal demons and exorcise the evil memories that bedevil him. Can he ever recapture the simple, guiltless pleasure of watching Magpies and Sunsets, forgiving the past and laying its ghost once and for all?

In a magnificently crafted and courageous book, Neil Marr makes no concessions to the English language as he throws his reader into the deep end of heavy, rough, tough dialect. A delight for all Scots, a journey of adventure for millions of expatriate Caledonians around the world and a challenge to all Sassenachs!
Paperback ISBN 1-904492-29-0

BeWrite Books